RED ROOM

Extreme Horror

Ash Ericmore

Written by: Ash Ericmore

Copyright © 2023 Ash Ericmore

All Rights Reserved. This is a work of fiction. No part of this publication may be reproduced, distributed, or transmitted in any form or by any means, except in the case of brief quotations embodied in critical reviews.

ISBN: 9798389510456

WITH SPECIAL THANKS TO

CHRISTINA PFEIFFER, AUGUST VAUGHN, JESSICA SHELLY, DONNA LATHAM, CHRISTOPHER RIDGE, BAMEBALLS, EDDIE GREENHAM, AND TIA WRIGHT

Want to see your name here? Check out

ko-fi.com/ashericmore/tiers

to find out how, as well as see all the other benefits of joining up.

Chapter 1

It feels like a burning sensation in the middle of the chest. Mike sat back in his computer chair, feet firmly flat on the floor, to stop that God damned pain in his hips. Between the two of them he felt like he was falling apart. "Jesus," he muttered. Fingers on the mouse. The browser closing. He was feeling like he was underwater, again. The unbearable feeling of loneliness. He wasn't alone. Far from it. He knew that. There were people in the world far worse off than he was. He could get in the car and go out. He could walk into town. He could pick up the phone. He had family. He had *friends*.

But he was solitary.

This job didn't help either.

He looked at the phone and waited, expecting it to ring. Getting laid off from his job in the factory some months ago, he'd thought working from home, a call centre worker for lack of a better term, was a fantastic idea.

Until he was doing it.

Answer the phone. Company name. Yada-yada. Then follow the instructions on the screen without fail. Even if it didn't make any sense. Printers. They were the fucking worst. Get some schmoe on the phone saying their printer had stopped working, and sure, the instructions made sense, and they followed them without question. *Is there a little light on the power button? No? Well, let's see if it's plugged in shall we?* Always talk like we're fixing it together. Placate the schmoe.

But then there were others. Dudette on the phone says she works in the IT department of some financial company, and the thing doesn't work *out the box*.

Is there a little light on the power button?

You could hear them sigh. *Fucking hell*, they're thinking. Dance the dance. They usually say something like, I've been doing this for fifteen years—my guy, it *doesn't work*. I just want a returns number. And then you have to beg. *Please, could you just tell me, is there a light on the power button?* Because the screen with the questions on won't change until you click the button on the bottom of the screen. Yes or No. And you know after fifteen questions (which is on a premium rate phone number, so this pointless support call is making your company money) you'll get the returns number that you know the woman knows she needs, but you can't get there… yet. And you can't just click quickly though the answers to skip to the returns number, because if you do, they who watch you work will see that you didn't have enough time to ask the questions and you'll be in the shit for skipping the questions and costing the company the premium rate call. But they won't say that.

No.

They'll say you didn't do your due diligence with the customer and perhaps you could have rectified the issue and gotten the printer working and saved the customer money in the long run. Time and money.

Bad employee.

And then your three month trial period gets extended to six months and they who watch you work spend more time watching you work, because you're an insolent little child who can't do as the company tells you.

The phone rings.

And, you have to answer the phone within three rings or you're in the shit for that. Heaven forbid you needed a second piss break in the morning, and had already used up your allotted piss break time and so had to answer the call with your cock in your hand.

Mike answered the phone, ignoring the burning pain in his chest, and that feeling of drowning, the weightlessness coming from it.

He should have gotten another job out there, in the world somewhere, instead of there. In his flat. Staring at the wall.

At least there would be other people.

But he wouldn't be able to answer the calls with his cock in hand. He droned out the spiel from the screen. Didn't really need to look at the screen, not for this first bit. Always the same. His personal laptop on the desk next to the work one. Thinking in the back of his mind about opening the browser on it again.

Surfing while he worked.

If he did it on that laptop, they couldn't see. Didn't know.

Not as long as he answered the calls within three rings.

Chapter 2

A sigh. He was on the last call. Just finishing up. It was gone the time he was supposed to finish. That was how it worked. He clocked off at four-thirty. If a call came in at four twenty-nine, he was stuck on it until the call was finished. Usually fifteen minutes. Sometimes less. He was just saying his goodbye bullshit speech from the screen—he could tell that they'd bored with the call, but were far too British to just hang up—and so it went on. And on.

Then, call closed.

Mike logged off the work laptop. Closed the lid. Looked at Ebay on his own laptop. He'd been looking at collectable figurines of Manga characters while the customer had pointlessly gone to find a lint-free damp cloth to run over the runners of the printer, while both he and the IT guy new that the motor was fucked. Some of those Manga girl figures were pretty racy. You know?

He sighed. Pulled the lid of his laptop closed. He should take a few minutes from the screen. Picked up his phone, swiped it open and held his thumb over the messages from his girl. She was still at work. Not the right time to text her. He was also feeling a little needy. *Needy cunt*. It was in his head. He was fine. *Everything was fine.*

He spun around in his chair, away from the desk, stood. His hip hurt. Always did when he first stood up. Needed a better chair. This one was fine when he was working at work. Now he was sitting in the damned thing for fucking eight hours a day, sometimes longer. His posture fucking sucked. His desk fucking ...

Spinning to face the front door, he walked over, pushed his feet in his trainers. Still laced. Never undid the laces. Then he pulled the door open, taking his jacket from the hook. Out. Into the hallway.

Old converted two up, two down house. There was a small hallway outside his front door. The door to the flat upstairs on his left, door out to the street on his right. Flat upstairs had a hooker living up there.

That was speculation. Fuck, he'd never even seen her, but it fucking well sounded like she was on the game. He shook his head, and turned to the right. Out the front door.

The evening was darker than he was used to. Stupid fucking daylight savings bullshit. Down a few steps to the path. He looked down through the window of the basement flat. Light on in there. There were a couple of young guys living there. Wasn't sure what their story was. Didn't care much, either. They were quiet. That was all Mike cared about.

The building opposite was the sorting office for the area. Big fuck off red brick building. It meant the road was busy, but at least there were no street parties and shit when there was a coronation or something. The council never closed the road.

He sniffed in the air. It was chilled, but not cold. Halloween soon, so there was a constant damp in the air, but not cold-cold. To the right, about five minutes was the town centre, to the left, another five minutes was a massive park. It was a good place to live from that point of view. He turned towards the town.

Probably shouldn't spend any money, but what the hell? He wandered.

Wasn't out for the exercise. He just wanted to walk out the pain in his hip and get some fresh air. He sidestepped the dog shit on the path. Dirty fuckers. He understood, sure, not wanting to pick up dog shit, but also, *fuck you*. You chose to have a fucking dog. He went to the crossroads, across, passing the church on the right. No idea what sort of church it was. They all looked very much the same. He'd not been in one since his old work wife got married. Had no intention of going into one again.

Towards the clocktower. Other side of the road, the old printworks that had been empty for years had been ripped to pieces and an art gallery stood there now. This town didn't need an art gallery. Not another fucking one, that was for sure. At the corner he stopped and leant against the railings that surrounded the traffic lights. Stopped people from wandering out into the flow of the traffic. Stretched his back, arching it. Bloke smoking a joint walked by, and Mike caught a breath of his stank. It had been a while. The urge to smoke tobacco was long gone, but the gear still smelled good. He could still taste it sometimes. Couldn't fucking afford it now. He looked, watching the dude walk away, down the hill towards the old town. Brazen. Smoking a joint in the street like that. Big fuck off guy. Leather jacket. Long one. Like the Matrix. Probably thought he was too cool to get nailed by the law.

Mike shook his head, looking out into the traffic. The library on the other side, diagonally. Court house. Lovely town centre. He pushed himself from the railings and crossed on the lights. Running across, well, half jog, to the centre island and then slow walk after. Onto the other side, through the bus stops, passing the Greek place that was still trying to open up. Across the top of the high street, and there he stood. Leaning against the wall. A few people coming and going, but it was the end of the day. The shops starting to close up—what little shops hadn't been chased out of the high street—and people going home. He looked out, down the hill, past the clocktower, to the beach. Too cold for anyone to be there. The ocean lapping at the sand. The arcades opposite, desolate. He was surprised they stayed open at all. People these days didn't seem interested. He could see why, himself. The last time he'd walked into the arcade, the machines were a pound, sometimes more, for a go. You could buy a second hand Xbox 360 for thirty quid. With games. Why waste your money on shit like this?

He snorted out a laugh, little grimace. Hands pushed in his pockets, curling them. Colder there, facing the water. Mike turned back.

He headed down the high street towards the old town. Walk a small circle and then back to the flat. Maybe by then Bree would have finished work and he could text her.

The bloke from the Premier shop down the road walked by, and he half-heartedly nodded to Mike like he wasn't sure if they were supposed to know each other. It was okay. Mike smiled, grunting some (also half-arsed) response and the two men passed. Like they'd stood near each other in the urinals.

Chapter 3

Bree was waiting for it. Liam Tranking was walking around the office. He was the boss's son. Of course. He was wearing a suit that was far too expensive for someone like him. And he was touching the desks of each of the employees. The women's ones, actually. Nothing else. Just walking by, saying one, maybe two words, and then just running his fingers over the side of the desk, like he was checking for dust.

"Hey, Bree Cheese," he said.

And *there it was*.

The swoosh of the fingers along the desk. And he was gone. At least it only took a few seconds. She smiled up at him—in his general direction—ignoring the fact that he wasn't looking at her. Just letting him pass on by, like the flu. When he stopped. Hand held pregnant to the side, and turned.

"Actually," he said, "could I see you in my office?" It wasn't a question.

"Now?" Bree asked.

"Now," he said. Then he continued walking.

Fuck. Bree sucked air in and stood, following him down the open plan office. She glanced at Leslie on the next desk along, her eyebrows up, mouth pulled down. No idea? Maybe that was what she was trying to convey? Maybe. Bree didn't need to be in trouble. She needed a job and there weren't many about at the moment, not that paid enough to have a flat *and* a life.

What had she done to deserve it? Her mind raced back through the accounts she had run this month. The company ran other company's payroll systems. It was just number crunching. Bullshit work, but easy, and paid, and she rarely had to stay late, which was a plus.

She was sure she hadn't done anything stupid.

Liam turned off the open plan main office into his own. It was a small room, but he seemed impressed with it. He was always impressed with himself. The room was walled on three sides with a large window on the last, looming over the workers. Like he was *the man*, and they were a typing pool, and this was the eighties.

As she reached the window, she saw that he'd turned around in the room, and was watching through the window. She passed him entering the office. Waiting, nervous, for instruction.

"Shut the door," he said, quietly.

Bree obliged without a word.

"Sit."

She did.

He stayed there, at the window.

Bree sat, uncomfortable in the silence for a moment, before turning in the chair and looking at him. He was still staring out at the workforce.

"Do you know what I had to do to get where I am today?" he asked, not moving from his vantage.

Be the boss's son? No. Couldn't say that, although it raised a smile on her lips. A quick one, gone before he could have possibly turned to see it. "No," she said.

He turned on his heels. Like a Nazi in a sitcom. "Anything," he said, now looking down at her. "I had to do anything that was expected of me." He stood there for a further second, over her, like he was trying to intimidate her. "Do you understand?"

She didn't. Not a fucking clue.

Liam turned back to the window and fiddled with the bit of plastic hung from the right of the window and the blinds lowered, closed.

The room a little darker.

God. What was going to happen now?

Liam flipped the lights on and the yellow glow of cheap lighting crackled, filling the room. He returned to the desk and sat. Opposite her, his hands flat on the desk.

He was wearing a three-piece suit. The sort of suit that would look so sexy on a man, tailored to fit perfectly. He'd be strong and commanding. It didn't work for Liam. He didn't have the body for it. He was neither big, nor shaped. Looked a little bit like a stick figure in a suit. A cheap suit. And the suit wasn't. It was all very conflicting, all caused by his … frame. She raised her eyebrows, a little smile. Politely saying with her face, "Well?"

"If you want to get ahead in the game, you have to give a little," he said.

It sounded like he was getting this shit from the internet. Or he'd watched too many films from the nineties about money and power. Mad men? Who knows. "Okay," she said, unsure of the right answer, or if indeed there was a question. She could smell something. Menthol. Cough drops. Mediciney. It had to be him.

"Look," he continued, "I like you, I really do, but you need to make more of an effort."

What? She looked him in the eye, tried not to waver, but she couldn't help but look down at herself. "What?" she said, looking back up.

He shook his head. "You're never the first here. Never the last out." He waved his hand roughly in her direction. "You're dowdy."

Bree was so taken aback by the statement that she didn't even think to call him a cunt. "What?" she said. Again.

"Dowdy. If you want to get a head you need to try a little harder. I mean, look at them." This time he waved to the window.

Bree looked at the window. She couldn't look at them. The blinds were closed. What the fuck was he talking about? What was happening? He wasn't firing her, was he? She didn't think so. She looked back at him, his hands, now back on the desk, flat. "How?" she said, confused.

"Don't be so ... *you*."

Bree's eyes widened. "Okay," she said. Maybe he was having a mental breakdown? Maybe that was it. "I can do that tomorrow."

"Good," he said, nodding. "Do that. I want you to come in early. Dressed to impress me. We'll have a breakfast meeting. How does that sound?"

She nodded. Dumbstruck.

"Good. See you at seven." Then he waved a dismissive hand, and she was allowed to go.

Bree got up and left the office without further word. What the fuck had just happened? She looked down herself vaguely as she wandered across the office floor. What was wrong with her clothes? *Was* it her clothes? Makeup? Hair? She looked at some of the other women in the office. There were about fifteen desks, more women than men, but not by many. They all looked like her ... didn't they?

Or was he suggesting that she might be in line for a promotion?

Fuck.

She should make an effort to come in early in the morning looking hot. Get that promotion. Chase it. Shit. Seven in the morning though? Was she supposed to bring breakfast? Was that how a breakfast meeting worked? She realised she'd wandered to a halt in the middle of the office. Staring into some middle distance. Felt like she was clutching pearls. She should go back and ask. More details. She looked back, and there was Liam standing in the doorway of his office.

Watching her.

She flashed him a smile and returned to her desk, shaking her head silently at Leslie whose face had a thousand questions on it. Not now, her head shake said. *Not now.*

She stared at her screen. Right. New dress. Had to be the first thing she needed. But she had to have it before morning.

Her phone vibrated on the desk.

That meant that she had to go shopping after work. She closed her eyes for a moment. But where? Fucking supermarkets were the only thing around there that would still be open. The whole fucking town was a shitbox these days. No. Finish up at five, jump into the car and head into Ashbury. The nearest city. Loads open there in the evening.

Her phone vibrated again.

What? she yelled in her head. She snatched the phone up, surreptitiously looking towards Liam's office, to make sure he wasn't standing there, watching her answer her personal phone. He was gone. Retreated back into the office to play on the internet, no doubt. Whispers were that he watched porn in there sometimes. She looked at the phone.

Mike. Two texts. *You okay?* And then *You free tonight?*

She shook her head. No. Not in the slightest. She slipped the phone down and looked at the time on her computer as she started to pound numbers into boxes again. It was barely five. He should know better than to text.

Leslie was logging off her machine.

Yes. Work an extra few minutes. That'll help. Bree nodded at her as she stood, swinging her coat over her shoulders. "What was that all about?" she hissed, making sure no one else was near her.

Bree shrugged. "I'll have to tell you later," she whispered, her attention firmly on the screen.

Leslie just shrugged it off, took her bag and left.

Bree side-eyed her as she went, watching half the staff pack up and leave. Waiting until most of them had gone, before even starting to close her applications down. One eye on the office. Her mind on shopping. She pushed her chair back and stood, quickly surveying the people still working. She knew most of them. They weren't a threat to her promotion. That was for sure. Her eyes floated on Paul for a moment. Apart from him. He was a fucking butt cheese. Arse licker. Whatever. He hadn't been called into the office though had he?

She snorted, and one of the women—Gina, she thought—looked over to her.

Bree ignored it, and continued. Pulled her jacket off the back of the chair and headed out the office door. There were three people at the lift, so she skipped that and hit the stairs.

The stairwell at the back of the building was pretty much a fire escape, so there was no carpet, or paint on the walls, just a gloomy, but wide, set of concrete steps rolling in an angular spiral down floor after floor. She almost skipped down them to the bottom.

Opening the door, out in the basement car park.

She reached her car before the people waiting at the lift came out the doors. Losers. She smiled to herself and beeped her car open. Slipped into the front seat and dropped her bag on the passenger side. Locked the car doors before starting the engine.

Her phone buzzed again, vibrating in her bag.

She picked it up and looked at it.

Mike.

Again. Shit. She stared at the screen for a moment. Her thumb rolled in a little circle while she decided whether or not to reply. She had more important things to do. And she wasn't sure if she cared if he understood or not.

Which wasn't a good thing, she supposed.

She pushed the phone back in her bag, engine on, she curled around looking behind her, reversing out the space.

Now Streaming

Gel strode to the centre of the room, a high price 'Sexy S.S.' uniform on. Barely covered her curved body. She stood, facing away from the camera. Give them one of the things they want from the show. *One of.* It was a joke between her and Raymond. The guy behind the camera. He was sitting on the other side, watching her with one eye, the screen with the other. Middle of the screen had her arse framed in it. The rest of the screen was circled with the cameras of the viewers.

They weren't allowed to watch if they didn't have a camera on them. So they were captured in the moment, the same as everything else.

They couldn't see each other. They didn't need to. They didn't even know that someone was watching. But they *did* know that they were being filmed. And apparently none of them cared. One of the little screenshots showed a torso. No face. Raymond typed into the chat window, "Show face, or I'm blocking."

The dude reached forward and manipulated his camera. Middle aged guy. Chat window just returned, "Sorry." He had a salt and pepper beard. Wearing a suit. Looked like he was sitting in a high powered corner suite in a tower block. Could have been anywhere in the world. It was light, behind him, out the window.

Dark where Raymond was.

Gel bent forward. Her panties were stained wet. All for the camera.

Some of them typed frantically into the chat window, messages popping up left and right. Raymond ignored them. You don't get a say until the show has started. And this wasn't the show. He took a look himself though, over the screen. At the real thing. "Nice," he said.

Gel looked back at him, a wide grin. She had a wide mouth. Like Julia Roberts. Big. Sexy. Raymond grinned back, and she could tell what he was thinking.

"Laters, Baby," she said. Already had a German accent going.

He hoped she'd keep that on *laters*, while she took off everything else. Blinking away the thought of fucking her, he turned his eyes back to the screen. Let out a wry little laugh. "You should stand back up. I think you're going to get the crowd going early."

Her laugh joined his, and she straightened, stepping out the range of the camera, and returned to him, behind the scenes. "Jesus," she said, pointing at one of the small screens. Guy had a rock solid hard on, completely visible, face in shot too.

"You sure you don't want to start blackmailing these fuckers?"

She snorted. "It's not good business to fire shots at the customers."

"Word's hardly likely to get around, is it?"

She glanced at him, unsure if he was serious or not. "You want a price on your head?" she asked. "Pissing off these fucks?"

He rolled his eyes, and glanced from the screen to her. "I'm fucking joking," he said. Dry. Like he was trying to cover his tracks.

"Besides," she said, crossing the room off camera, "give them what they want and we're hardly going hungry, are we?"

He nodded, eyes still on the screen. There was a woman in the top left. He'd dragged her little screen up there to keep an eye on her. It was unusual to see a woman in the audience. Wanted to see if she a) dropped off as soon as she realised what she'd paid for, b) looked like she was something she shouldn't be—fucking Interpol, Counter-something, you know the types, or c) she was a fucking freak. Raymond thought he could probably tell by the faces, the actions. The guy in the suit. He was a freak. The guy with the stiffy—he was too. It was the people with nothing behind them. The people that were being too careful. They were the ones you had to watch.

It was like when you spoke to a girl on the phone. Like a young one. The feds were good at it, but they would try to manipulate you into instigating everything. So it wasn't entrapment. And if you were wise on it, then you could spot them. Real girls, the ones looking to hook up with an older man, they were always right up for it. All about the dick. Never got that far, of course. Raymond only got them for *this*.

"Ready?" Gel asked.

Raymond glanced at her. He pressed a few buttons and the feed of the room was replaced with the pictures of today's showpiece. Angela, her name was. That was on the screen, along with three stills of her, various states of undress, going from one to the next. Showing everything. She said she was twenty-one, but when Raymond met her he thought she might have been nearer eighteen. Maybe a year either way.

The American cheerleader outfit she was wearing

was put on her after she was unconscious. Something for the customers to look at. Best not to show her in the clothes she was taken in, just in case photos circulate.

Grabbing girls was easier these days. Thanks *dating apps*.

Raymond's eye's flicked around the screen as several people disconnected. Mostly it was the regulars. Understandable. Angela was a blonde. Big tits. But she looked cheap in the face. Like she'd been around the block, even for a young 'un. Not everyone wanted that. His eyes slipped up to the woman in the corner. Still there. She'd leaned in to look at the photos closer. Could be the law, trying to identify a victim. Could be getting off on it. Raymond smiled. He'd work it out soon enough.

The guy rocking the hard-on was stroking it.

Raymond shook his head. Hopefully he had a deep wallet or was ready to wait.

Gel, having left the room, suddenly pushed back in, through the doors. Pushing a wheelchair. Angela sat in it. Her head was lolling backward, completely out of it. Gel pushed her to the centre of the feed, an x marking the spot on the floor. She toed the lock on the chair, locking the wheels in place. Then she left the feed window.

Raymond pressed some more buttons and the screen changed from the photos—the last one of Angela naked, on the floor, hands above her head, legs spread. It would have been sexy if she'd been aware of it. But it was just a glamour shot. So they could see it all. No one liked surprises. Before, when they did headshots only, one dude had paid good shit to see her panties cut off her, and when he saw she was shaven, he'd gone ape shit on the feed. Fucking threw Raymond for a loop, trying to pacify him, and keep the auction going at the same time. Since then, there were no surprises.

The feed filled the screen, and the crowd went wild. Stroker started getting a little harder. Faces got closer to screens. Some of those in darker rooms, the bright light of the screen contrasting out their faces with white, so close, Raymond wondered if they were licking their screens. Fucking hell. At least one of them probably was. He looked to the top corner. The woman had disconnected. Couldn't be the law, she'd left too early. Couldn't be an innocent, either, she'd been there too long. Must have seen something she didn't like.

Shame.

Raymond would have liked to see her get off on it. Maybe next time.

He glanced up at Angela. Her head rolled slightly. She was coming around. He tapped the keyboard and a timer started on the screen. He saw faces light up in excitement. The regulars that were still there were used to sometimes waiting thirty minutes or far more for this. One disconnected. He was an older man. His old woman had probably called him for dinner. Raymond smiled. It was certainly a diverse lot.

"Going for a pee," Gel said.

Raymond glanced up at her, leaving the room. Before he turned his attention to the customers. Eyed around them quickly at first, discounting the regulars. There was a guy watching, intently, sure, but his mouth was moving. Raymond didn't insist access to their mics—fuck, hearing them was the last thing he wanted—but he killed the guys connection anyway. Blacklisted his username. He was either a cop, or he was talking on the phone while waiting, and that was damned right disrespectful. No one else was doing it. Raymond watched the guy with the hard-on. Edging himself. Interesting to get that far along, before the show started, but each to their own. He raised an eyebrow. Didn't really want to see that culmination of activity, particularly. Eyes on the next one. Young guy. He was sitting back. Calm, collected. He looked like he might be psychotic. Raymond grinned. To be honest, most of them probably were. It went with the territory.

Angela let out a long, wheezing groan. Head rolling, she was trying to straighten in the chair.

"She's waking up," he shouted through to the next room.

"Coming." Gel came back through the door.

"Find a toilet?"

She giggled, "I pissed on the floor. Even if I'd found one, I ain't sitting on it."

Raymond wished he had eyes on that. Damn. He looked from her to the screen. *They'd* probably pay extra for it. Watching her pee on the meat. He picked up his pencil and scribbled it on his pad. Pee on the meat.

"Ready?" she asked, looking from Angela to Raymond.

Raymond studied Angela. "Couple of minutes," he said, quietly.

Gel sighed. Not wanting to wait. "Fine. I'll pack a bag." Then she left the room again.

Always so impatient. Raymond flicked his look from the door to the meat to the screens. The clients seemed raring to go. Timer almost out. Meat almost awake. Gel would pack up one of their bags now. When they'd finished, they'd do the rest. It wasn't like they would tidy up after themselves or anything. Every show from a different location. Leave the body behind for someone—or no one on a couple of occasions—to find and report later. Neither of them had so much as a parking fine. Forensics didn't matter. When they got caught—if they got caught—they'd both go down for life anyway.

So just mosey around the country. Making money, selling death. Streamed live from some abandoned factory, or warehouse, or whatever. You pay to play.

Gel came back in. She watched Angela for a second. "Ah," she said, knowing she was about ready. "I've done the bag. Ten minutes out there and we should be clear."

Ten minutes was about all it took for him to pack up the cameras and the laptop, the wireless stuff—satellite connection—that sort of shit. "Good," he said. "So, ready?" He glanced over the screen again. Another couple had disconnected, boring of the short wait, perhaps. He killed the timer.

Sent a message to all the clients.

Begin.

There was a moment, the same at the beginning of most of these—auctions wasn't the right word, but it would do—auctions, where there was a lull where it appeared everyone was waiting for someone else to start.

Then, usually one of the bigger players chimed in with something small. Raymond was pretty sure that some of the big boys were almost as interested in what the young bloods wanted as sating their own needs, wants. The older man. In the corner office. He put in first.

Bids—for lack of a better word—were visible to

all. He typed in the message: *Let's see some goods then. Clothing, whatever I get for 500.*

Raymond relayed the message to Gel. Gel walked on camera for the first time since she'd shown her arse. She walked over to Angela. Looked down on her. She smiled into the girl's face. Angela was semi awake now. Enough to slowly put two and two together, but until she saw Gel, hadn't started to panic.

She looked at Gel for a moment. Then, like a light switch coming on, she screamed. She started to twist and turn and yank and cry. Like every flood gate opening at once. Gel shushed her, gently, like a mum. "Shh, sh, sh, sh." She smiled, warm. Quietly, too quietly for the clients to hear, she said, "There's no use in trying to free yourself. You can't. You might as well sit back and enjoy." The grin got wider and Gel stood back, just for a second. The words having the desired effect.

Angela screamed louder, her hands and feet braced into the chair with mental asylum quality belts. She looked around wildly. Looked at Raymond, begging suddenly. "Please," she screamed, "I won't say anything."

Like Raymond might have a change of heart. Oh, right-o then. Best let you go.

Pfft.

She looked at her wrists, able to twist them and turn them, but never get them more than an inch or so from the arms of the chair. She looked wildly down at the costume she was in. "What?" the word eeking from her mouth, slow. Like some dawning realization that she was totally and utterly fucked.

Gel stepped back in, knife in hand and cut the top open, up the centre, Angela naked beneath. Even with her squirming like a cat, Gel was careful not to nick the flesh. That cost extra. She flicked the torn material open and let her breasts be seen clearly by the cameras first, then she grabbed a handful and squeezed like she was some pimp showing off the product. She stepped back.

"That enough?" Raymond asked. "Five hundred."

Gel shrugged. She flashed him a wink.

Raymond looked back at the messages. Naked guy was still edging himself. He only had a few more minutes and then Raymond'd block him. This wasn't a wank show, not unless you were willing to pay. Some fuckboy typed in: *Cut her tits off. 10.*

Raymond tossed him from the show, but didn't block him. He could come back another time, maybe when he was grown up enough to understand the game. He looked at the screen, eyes darting from the messages to the screens of the clients. A lot of sitting, waiting. Raymond sighed, quiet. He glanced up to Gel. "Well?" she mouthed. He shrugged. He typed into the global chat, "Bids, or we close the room."

The first guy, again. Poor fucker was going to carry the whole auction if he wasn't careful. Typed in: Rest of the clothes. 500.

Raymond smiled.

Chapter 4

The pub was one of those old fashioned things. Down near the station. Had small round tables everywhere and baby stools instead of chairs. It had a feel of the eighties about it. The woman behind the bar was standing somewhat flaccidly. Watching Vic, sitting on the stool in the middle of the room. Book in one hand, phone in the other. His eyes going between the two of them. "Not saying much this evening."

Vic's eyes flicked to the time on the phone, then he looked up at her. He smiled. "Sorry. Been a week."

She shook her head. "You can always tell me."

He could. He sort of knew that. But he just wasn't that person. It was only five. He'd finished work an hour ago, home. Change. Down to the pub for a quick couple, before going back home. To sit alone. Laura was a friend of sorts. She was always on at that time. Nice girl. He liked her. He half wanted to ask her out. Had no idea how to. Fuck it. He didn't know how to talk to girls at all. Never had done. Not since he'd been at school. He glanced over to her. She was cleaning something behind the bar. Not really wanting to know what was wrong with him. Or was it because she was at work, and she had to look busy?

No. Probably not wanting to know.

That was more likely.

He looked back at the book. It was some science

fiction horror thing he'd picked up at the charity shop down on Winchester street, last Saturday. He was still trying to get into it, refusing to give up. He flipped it closed with a thwap, and stuffed it in his carrier bag, at his feet, his attention going to the phone instead. He looked at the picture of the girl, Debbie, on the screen. Said she was local. Within five miles. She was pretty. Funny, in her bio. His eyes went back to the picture. Long brown hair. She was wearing glasses in one shot—a selfie—camera up above her, finger in her lips. Made her look like she was sucking your cock. By design, he was sure. She wasn't going to like him. She was clearly all about hunks and cock. And he was neither a hunk, nor was he hung. He felt his face burn a little red. Fuck it. He looked up. Laura was staring at him. She looked away when he looked up.

Probably looking at something else.

He looked back at Debbie. She had some more photos there, that you could only see if you had a premium membership. He didn't. Wasn't going to either. The luck he'd had on this thing, it was little more than window shopping. No one ever checked the interested box for him. He checked the interested box for Debbie. She would see he had, then ignore him. Just like all the others.

Why none of these women were interested in him, he didn't know. Fuck. He thumbed the screen across to the next one. She was red haired. He looked at her photos. Back to the bio, quickly. Name was Morgan. That sounded made up, but whatever. He returned his gaze to her photos. She was in a swimsuit in the first one. Had a finger hiked under the top of it, and was pulling it down. Increasing the size of her cleavage, to her ample chest. Big toothy smile.

Camera coming down at that blowjob angle again. Vic sighed.

"You okay?"

He jumped. Laura was almost standing over him. He quickly turned his phone. Looked up at her. "Of course," he said. "Fine." He picked up his pint and took a sip. He liked to drink quicker than this, but the beer there was expensive. He was only in there, because it was quiet. He didn't particularly like crowds. He'd go home after this pint, pick up some cider on the way back and drink that in front of the TV. Put a film on maybe.

Horror? Probably horror.

Laura pulled her mouth to a thin-lipped half-smile and then walked off, back across the bar.

Vic turned his phone over and looked at … checked the name … Morgan, again. He looked at the next photo. She was head and shoulders only in that one. Cut off carefully to look like she was naked. Probably wasn't. Just teasing. The next. Shot at some beach. Didn't look like the beaches in England. Looked more like the continent. Ibiza or something. The seaside. Hadn't visited the seaside in years. Maybe he should try that. Go to the seaside and meet someone across the table in a fish and chip shop. Their eyes meeting. Fingers touching as they both reached for the vinegar.

He giggled. Shut himself up. Glanced to Laura. Then turned his attention back to Morgan. Had a nice arse in the beach shot. Probably why she chose it. Again, though, this was getting him nowhere. He put a check in the interested box.

Flicked the button on the side of the phone and stuffed it in his pocket. He chugged the last fifth of the pint as he stood. Turned. "I'm off," he said, a light little wobble. Stood up too quickly.

"Your bag," she said.

Vic bent and picked it up. "Cheers," he said. One last glance, half-smile, to the door. Out.

The evening was dark. Getting late in the year. The wind was hard, but it wasn't cold. He closed his eyes for a second. Two thoughts. The first was Morgan. He could imagine what she looked like under the swimsuit. Round breasts. Couldn't imagine their taste. Not yet. Maybe later. The second thought was a pang, a longing, for a cigarette. Had quit some months ago. He was expecting the want to have fucked off by now, but no. No chance. His phone buzzed in his pocket.

He pulled it out and looked at it. Somewhere in the back of his mind it was Morgan, matching with him. He'd get to find out what she tasted like. He snorted. A notification from the Gas Board about his monthly bill.

Much   more   likely   than   a   match.

Chapter 5

Mike was sitting at his computer, had a video playing. Something about some fucker who was inciting unrest on social media by encouraging misogynistic behaviour. He had his finger on the spacebar, and was gently pushing it down. About halfway down, the video paused, and keeping pushing, when the bar reached the bottom, the video unpaused, and Mike let his finger slip off it, releasing it.

Rinse and repeat.

He wasn't paying much attention to the video. It was just noise. Filling the space. The void. He looked across to the TV. He could go and put that on. Maybe that would hold his attention more. There was a can of beer in the fridge, but he didn't feel like it. He should eat, but he didn't feel like it. That burning sensation was in his chest again. His head was full of monsters. Bree hadn't text him back, and she must have left work by now. She'd always left work by now.

He slipped his hand across the desk and left the video to continue to play. Got up and went to the kitchen. The flat wasn't big, but it was big enough. Enough for him, and to entertain on occasion. He needed to have his parents over for coffee or something again, but he hadn't gotten around to it, or hadn't bothered. Didn't want to do shit? He stopped in the hallway, looking through into the kitchen.

There was shit piled in the sink. "Fuck," he whispered. He went and picked through it to find a mug, before rinsing cold water over it and pushing it on the side. He opened the fridge and pulled out a milkshake carton. Poured himself one. He looked at the sink. He could smell it. Or maybe that was the overflowing garbage. The sugar in the milkshake woke his taste buds. Made him want some chocolate. Snorting out a laugh, he looked down at himself. Fucking belly tight against his t-shirt. This one used to fit. He was sure of it. Pulled his phone out his pocket and thumbed it, making sure he hadn't missed her text message.

Left the kitchen, walked the rest of the hallway. Looked in the bedroom. Clothes on the floor. Bed was clean though. Just in case. He looked at his feet. He'd kicked his shoes off when he'd gotten back from the walk. They were to the side of the front door. He tried to remember when the last time they'd had sex was. Closed his eyes. He could remember it—the actions, her body—but he couldn't remember when it was. Last week? Tuesday? She'd come over at the weekend, hadn't she? Fuck. Working from home, everything was fucking blending together.

He turned back to the living room.

The video had changed. It was playing some movie review. Mike went and sat on the arm of the sofa. The room could use vacuuming. It smelled a little like he had a cat, but he didn't. A sudden flourish of rain on the window got his attention. He sloped into the bay and looked out. The path only feet from him. People hurrying by, as surprised as he was by the shower.

Then it stopped as suddenly as it started.

The video changed again on the laptop, playing to

itself. One of those fucking top ten lists. He turned and looked at the screen. Could barely make it out from that distance. Half of the living room—by the window—made up to be a living room, but the far side, an office. His laptop on the desk in the corner. It was something about the dark corners of the internet. He slumped down onto the sofa and pulled his phone. Again, nothing. He thumbed his messages. He should text her again. What if something had happened to her? Maybe she was in an accident or something. What fucking good would texting her do then? Hanging upside down in the car in a ditch. *Hold on, better text Mikey back.*

But, when she was better, he could show her the messages. Show her how super caring he was, that he was worried. Get some of those sweet brownie points.

He let the phone rest back, and took a sip of his milkshake. It was a bit cunty to do it for that reason, though, wasn't it? It was. The internal conversation didn't stop him from keeping his thumb there, until he decided what to do.

Head thumping. Not a headache. Just felt like his brain was getting bigger, filling the space. That didn't make sense. That burning feeling in his chest.

Depression, maybe that was what it was. Loneliness.

C H A P T E R   6

Bree ignored the phone going again. It was getting dark and she hadn't even begun to choose what shop to hit. She was still sitting in her car. When she'd left town the weather was fine. Here in the city, it was overcast. Spitting with rain. She was waiting to see if it was going to shit down, or stop. It made a difference to her next move.

The rain seemed unperturbed and just wanted to continue as was.

Well, that was just fine, then. She grabbed her bag from the passenger seat and pushed herself out the car, slamming the door as she hurried off towards the shops. Dodging the drops, as she went. Into the first large department store she saw.

That would be fine, she thought. Just something appropriate for work, but not dowdy. She looked down herself again—for possibly the four hundredth time that evening—and frowned, as she brushed the drops of water from her coat.

The store smelled like perfume.

She looked up at the signage. It was getting late, and she didn't want to spend the whole night in there. Hit the escalators to get to the next floor.

Her phone went ... again. She stood, watching out over the floor that disappeared below her as she rose, holding in a scowl. Fucking hell. She pushed her hand in her bag and pulled out the thing and stared at it, swallowing back the anger. Jesus Christ it had only been like twenty four hours since she'd seen him. She felt like he had her on a fucking string. Her heart started to increase in speed. Face screwed up as she looked at the phone. Damn it.

Bree stepped off the escalator and headed towards the suits.

Mike walked between the kitchen and the bedroom again. He looked in the bathroom. The shower needed cleaning. He turned back to the living room. Looked at the laptop. The video had stopped itself while he wasn't watching. Some message on the screen asking if he was still watching or if he'd died somewhere along the way.

He slumped with the beer from the fridge in his hand. The video was paused in the middle of what looked like one of those real world documentary things. Like a serial killer doc, or something. He pushed on the spacebar again, and the video started. Some Irish guy. Smooth voice. He was talking about some unsolved mystery in York. Mike flicked the ring pull on the can. York. Where the fuck was that? Up north, obviously, but geography wasn't his strong suit. Had difficulty finding his arsehole sometimes. He pulled the can, opening it with a *fiiiish*. Then he pushed it to one side, leaving the video running and pulled up Google Maps. York was sort of middle north. Before Scotland. He closed the map and returned to the video. He'll have forgotten where it was in what … ten minutes?

He sipped the beer. Acrid and dry. It tasted like … beer. The thing was, Mike wasn't much of a drinker, and while someone who knew what they were talking about would have said that it was full bodied, with hoppy aromas from an earthy soil, Mike said it tasted like beer. And not a particularly good one, either. Some chick he'd been forced into conversation with—by her—when he was in the off licence the other day had persuaded him that this shit was the dog's bollocks, and he should buy some. He should have known she was talking out her arse, because she was buying white fucking cider. And the dude on the counter was reading porn. He'd already made a mental note not to go back in there, because of him, but having now tasted the beer, he certainly didn't want to bump into her again.

He looked from the lip of the can to the screen, then to his phone. Dismissed all of it, except the video, and the agitated feeling of emptiness in his shoulders, and leant back in the chair.

The Irish guy was murmuring something about a body being found in an old unused school. He had a calming voice. Gentle. Serene. Mike closed his eyes and listened to him. Listened to his voice, rather than the words, toyed blindly with the can, his finger wrapping around its coolness, condensation dampening his fingers as he stroked them around the metal. A long draw of breath in.

How could she be ignoring him? He opened his eyes again, the image of Bree's face suddenly the only thing he could see in the darkness. How? Why? He popped the beer can under his fingers, pushing the tin in, and then releasing it. She was going to fucking leave him, wasn't she? He tasted the bitter liquid, looked disdainfully at the can and then dropped his attention back to the video.

The school was in Wales. Mike focussed. What? *Damn it*. He should have been paying more attention. He looked at the mouse. It was out of reach and therefore rewinding the video was impossible. So he focussed on the stream and tried to follow from where he was.

But his mind wouldn't leave her alone.

Bree pushed the hanger back on the rail from where it had come from. She wanted something that would impress him, but this shit was all so ... she made a small snorty noise. Fucking dowdy. She shook the word from her head. Maybe she was looking at this all wrong. All these fucking business suits and shit. Maybe she needed to make her own look. Maybe that would work. Something sexy, that she wouldn't dream of wearing to work, and then build on it. Like The Devil Wears Prada. But cheaper.

She didn't have any money worries, of course, but in the back of her mind, she was always conscious of the flow in and out of funds. Smart. Savvy. Call it what you want, but she *had* to be aware of such things or suddenly there was no money before the end of the month and her savings would suffer. It had taken her *years* to build up those. Living there, shit town nowhere, keeping everything ticking over, and putting cash in the bank for a rainy day. Finally getting it to four figures. Five. Then still going.

None of which was going to be a problem once she had a promotion.

So the risk was worth it. Buy something wild for this meeting. Prove the point. Sure, it would take maybe eight weeks for the promotion to come through and the pay to flow, but she'd manage. More nights in with pasta and sauce, less nights out with the girls and a cocktail.

Her mind flickered to Mike.

Shit. She had to decide what she was going to do

with him. She should let him off the hook. He was a nice guy, and she really did like him, but there was just something that didn't click. It could have been the physical side. It could have been that he was clearly a little troubled, and that he'd managed to line his life up with never having to go out.

He wasn't really all that much fun.

She sighed, and went from one section, through the underwear, and out into another. Completely different attire. More, slinky, appealing clothes. Sort of things she would look at if she was going to go somewhere swanky and then on, out afterward.

She could work with that.

C H A P T E R   7

Raymond pushed the laptop in the holdall, across the top of the wiring. Zipped it up. Lifted it down from the table he'd set up on, before pulling the second bag up, and pushing the cameras in first.

Gel returned from the other room. "Ready," she said.

"Give me five," he said. He gave her nothing more than a glance. "Here," he said. He pointed to the side of his face.

"Shit." She turned back to the other room. "I forgot my makeup bag." She stepped from that room into the next, and crouched next to the bag containing her uniform. She was now dressed in jeans, a t-shirt. She pulled the baby wipes from the side pocket and dragged one from the little pouch hole at the top. Wiping it against her face, she pulled it back and looked at it. Smeared blood red. "Fuck," she whispered. She got back up and returned to the main room. "Better?"

Raymond looked up from the bag, nodded, and then got back on with the last of the packing.

"Some weird ones tonight," Gel said absently. She stood outside of the pooled blood, looking at the meat.

"Aren't they weird every night?" Raymond said.

He was only half listening, she knew. She looked at the meat, her flesh getting colder now. When the blood dried and the corpse got colder, it changed colour, wasn't so shiny. The odour too, it went quickly from the coppery fragrance of blood to a smell not dissimilar to milk about to turn. Not quite turned. Just about to. The meat was about in the middle of the two places at the moment. Just drying off.

She glanced at the gape that used to be her vagina, torn open, blood drools hanging like Halloween ornaments from between her legs, the whole area, wrecked. Up, to the torn off skin of her belly. "I guess." She checked her feet, again, to make sure she wasn't near the pool. The last thing she needed was to have to wash her trainers before they left. It wasn't like this place had any running water.

"Had a couple of wankers," he said.

She glanced back at him. "Over me or her?"

"Bit of both."

She smiled. It was a nice feeling, anonymously turning men on. Men all over the world closing their eyes and stroking themselves to vinegar, all over the thought of you. Your wet panties up in their face. She wondered if they imagined what she smelled like, and if they did, what they thought she did. Dirt and grime. Slutty fucking used cunt. Or flowers and perfume. Each to their own. She didn't care.

Raymond had stopped and was staring at her all the while she stared off at nothing in some strange middle distance. "Ready," he said, zipping up the second bag.

She looked at him, vaguely at first, then grunted. She turned out of the room, followed by Raymond, grabbed the bags from there, and out to the car.

The beaten up, but still very legal to drive Mondeo was sitting there, back doors open where Gel had tossed her coat in, a few minutes before. She popped the boot, empty after the drive there, and dumped her bag in. Raymond followed suit, only more careful with the bag, because of the electronics.

"All the bitcoin transfers cleared before we were finished, so we're clean to head home." He used both hands and closed the boot, carefully.

Gel met his eyes and slipped in closer to him. Tip toed up and kissed him. He leant in, letting her, before kissing her back. She dropped back to her heels, her eyes still in his. "How long do you think?"

Raymond looked at his watch. Bottom lip suddenly poked out. "Three hours," he said, his tone rising at the end of the word hours, like he wasn't that sure. He wasn't, in all fairness. They'd been on the road for a lot longer than that coming there, but they'd stopped twice, before they had managed to catfish the meat into a meeting, and then grabbed her.

Gel rounded the car and pulled the passenger door open. "Good. Plenty of time for me to have a nap then." She slipped in.

Raymond shook his head. "One last check around," he called over his shoulder. He returned to the building and in. The outside of the building looked okay, but inside it was a fucking shell. He'd overlooked it several times when he was scoping out the area, trying to find a suitable location for the shoot. Thought it was still in use, or for sale of some shit. Somewhere he couldn't risk. Then he found out it was empty. And in all truth, it had been fucking perfect. He walked through the three rooms they'd used over the last few hours. Picked up the meat at around midnight. By the time they'd got her in the boot, over here, changed, photos taken ... it had been three in the morning before the auction had started.

He looked at his watch again. Just gone seven now. He stepped onto the shooting floor. Eyes keen on the floor. A glance at her. He had to admit she'd held on like a trooper. He absently kicked her fingers across the floor. No one likes it when they check out quickly.

On one occasion they'd barely made twenty grand. Not worth the risk for that.

Tonight, he hoped they'd hit nearer fifty. He'd have to do the conversions once they were back home. Returning to the room that Gel changed in, to the right of the door, he stopped, squinting into the shadows. He pulled his phone and turned on the torch. Across the floor, side to side. He crouched and pinched a small piece of gold. Held it into the light.

Earing.

"Fucking hell," he muttered. Leaving behind forensics was one thing, but evidence was something else. He stood, pushing the jewellery into his pocket. A shake of the head.

Out to the car. He shut the back door, and got in. Gel was staring into the distance, her eyelids hanging heavy. Started the engine. He gave her a quick glance. She didn't acknowledge it, or him. She was away with her thoughts. "Ready?" he asked.

She nodded, pushed her hand into her pocket and pulled out her pills. She turned the small white plastic bottle over, turning two of them out into her hand, before slapping them into her mouth. Taking a drink from the water bottle, wedged in the door.

She'd be asleep in a couple of minutes.

Raymond didn't mind. He liked to drive in the quiet. This time of the morning, even the motorways would be fairly dead. No music. Just his thoughts.

Chapter 8

Bree pulled the dress on, and then started to wrap other things around it, looking in the mirror on the back of the bedroom door. It was too early for this shit. In just the dress she looked like a fucking whore. What the fuck was she thinking? She glanced at the open wardrobe full of allegedly drab—no, *dowdy*—clothing, and then at the clock on the bedside table. It was five in the fucking morning, she'd had like, two hours sleep. Fucking Mike had text her at two—she thought, because she hadn't looked, but who the fuck else could it be?—this dress stank like a fucking Viking brothel, nothing looked right and she wanted to die. Or crawl back into bed. Either way right now would be fine. She slumped down to sit, the dress clinging onto her in lots of places she wished it wouldn't. Face fell into hands.

Jesus Christ.

She shook her head. Think logically. Breakfast meeting. Shit. She needed to get breakfast, too. *Breakfast from McDonalds* meeting. Big promotion on the table.

Why did she have nothing to wear?

Bree rubbed the ball of her hand into her eye. Right. Come on. No shit now. She stood up and looked herself down in the mirror. Then continued to pull things from the wardrobe and pull them on, and pull them off.

Until she was satisfied.

Well, as satisfied as she was going to be.

She stomped from the flat and into the hallway. To the front door of the building and looked through to the weather. Half-light at that time of the morning and she couldn't really see what was going on. So she opened the door and went to the road, to the car, parked in the curb.

Went through the drive thru.

Then when she got to work she pulled into the car park, all but empty under the building. There were one or two cars in there. Hopefully one of them was Liam's. She wasn't aware enough to know what he drove. She probably should know what the boss's son drove, but hey ho. She dragged the McDonald's bag from the car with her, trying to straighten her clothing as she walked, sure the food was going to be cold by the time she was in the meeting.

Fucking hell. She'd never had to attend a breakfast meeting before. Sounded fancy. She hit the stairs. Couldn't be bothered to wait for the lift. Up to her floor.

The lights in the main office were on. With nothing else on—the computers, phones—, she could hear them. She was never first—nowhere near first, ever, in fact—so she'd never seen the office empty before. She slipped her bag under her desk and looked down to see the light on in Liam's office.

Went down the middle of the office. The whole thing felt weird. She got to his door. Blinds were down. Light coming through the cracks. She knocked.

"Come."

She opened up. He was sitting at his desk. Sitting back, hand on the keyboard, like he was pretending to work. It was only seven in the morning. She was hardly expecting him to be working *hard*. Bree popped the food on the desk, between the two chairs, and he gestured for her to sit.

"Morning," he said. He ran an appraising eye over her clothes.

Bree noted that his mouth curled up at the corner. That was a good sign, right? So she sat, unloading McDonalds onto the desk between them. "I didn't know what you liked," she said.

Liam looked at the food, his face giving nothing away.

He certainly didn't seem happy to see it. Which was weird, because everyone loves McDonalds breakfast. Shit. What if she wasn't supposed to bring food? "So," she said. The word died a little in her mouth, with her having no way to know how to continue the sentence.

"So," he echoed. "I see you made an effort." His fingers flicked in her general direction and she assumed he was talking about her clothes.

She smiled her response. "Better?" she asked.

He didn't respond. "So," he said, again. "How do you think you're doing out there?" His eyes left her body for the first time and met her own.

"I think I'm doing okay," she began. She had thought that maybe he was going to want her to dole out some business stuff, and she'd sort of prepared, not knowing what sort of interview this was. The room had filled with the smell of McMuffins, and it was putting her off. "I think that some of the inputters could learn to work a little faster—the quality or their quality control could improve." She stumbled over the words a little. "I like to think that I do good." She stopped. He didn't say anything. Did he want more? She smiled at him. Trying to indicate that she'd finished.

Liam pushed himself from the desk. He looked at the food, then her, then up, behind her. "What do you think it takes to get ahead?"

"Anything," she said, echoing his words from the night previous. Prove she was listening.

"Anything," he said, like she hadn't spoken.

Bree was confused.

He tapped on the desk like he was knocking to come in, and then strode around behind her.

Her look didn't follow him, just stayed on the food she'd just bought, getting cold. Would it be all right for her to just start eating? She really had no idea of the proper way of doing these things. Listened, as she heard him fiddle with the blinds. Looking out, beyond his office to the main room.

Another blind rattle. Then he was standing next to her.

She looked up him. He was staring down at her.

Bree looked down herself, self-conscious. He could see down her dress from where he was standing. She was sure of it. She fiddled with the bust line of the thing, suddenly wishing she'd come more ... *dowdy*.

Then he touched her shoulder and she looked back up to him. "I could show you the ropes," he said. "Make your transition to management easier."

Promotion. She *knew* it.

"Of course," she said, hurriedly. "I want to learn." She was still looking up at him.

Liam's tongue darted from his mouth over his thin lips. Wetting them. "And what do you think should be your first step?"

Bree's eyes dropped. She thought for a second. "Well, if the rest of the clerks knew I was in the running, then I could take a more supervisory role out there." It was a brave play, she knew, suggesting an intermediary and immediate promotion. But her mum had always told her to shoot for the stars. This was it. *Negotiation of promotion.*

"Before that," he countered.

She looked up at him again. Fucking hell. The only things she could think of was telling Adrian that wore the brown suit in every day, that she was his supervisor now and ha ha ha fuck you, and the hash browns. They weren't even wrapped properly. In those little fry baggies, open, and getting soggy. He was staring down at her. Still. Thin lips in a smile now. A proper one.

He was enjoying this.

"What?" she said, the words coming out little more than a breath.

He shuffled, a little closer. He was really in her space now. Fingers still on her shoulder. Touching her flesh. He was so close to her, she could smell his perfume. It was *old* smelling. Like old man cologne. "Think ... hard," he said. "I need a thinker."

Fuck. "I—" she said.

"Yes."

"I—" The words weren't there. She needed something cool. Something game changing. Something that could change the productivity of the office like no other. "I—"

"*Yes.*" He was sounding super frustrated.

"I could reorganise the work flow to attain the best results." What? What the fuck did that even mean? It was business keyword bullshit. Jesus Christ. *Please don't ask me to go further into the nuts and bolts of that one.*

"In order to achieve that we would have to work

closely," he said.

"Yes," she said. The words were coming out of her mouth now without control. The brain had lost to some unforeseen revolt by the mouth. "The statistics at the end of the month would need a keen eye."

Liam sighed. "So, where should we start?"

Bree thought quickly. Taking control back from the mouth. Which was when she realised he was stroking her bare shoulder. That seemed a little over friendly, although he was talking about them working closely. She supposed they'd end up working later and such. She thought about Mike. Fuck. Clingy Mike wasn't going to like that. Although, all that did was pretty much seal his fate. She noted that he'd managed to get even closer. With the way he was standing and how she was sitting, he had all but pushed his groin into her face. Bree looked up him. Over her. Groin in her face. "Mr. Tranking," she said.

"Yes. I like that."

"What are you suggesting?"

"I'm not suggesting anything. We're brainstorming, aren't we?" His words were quiet. Whispers. Coming from his throat. "You need to think fast though."

"Brainstorming," she said. She was looking at his crotch. Didn't mean to be, but suddenly everything seemed obvious, really.

He didn't speak again. Seemed to be waiting for the cogs to finish going around.

She quietly asked herself, somewhere in the deep recesses of her mind, what she was really willing to do for a promotion. It wasn't a serious question. More a *what if...?* She looked up at Liam, and he was grinning down at her.

He made a noise with his mouth, goading sort of.

"Aaah?"

He thought this was okay. Bree looked at the McDonalds on the desk. Cold now, surely. To the crotch. The face. Back to the food.

"Well," he said. He shuffled back a little. "I think we're done here." His voice was steady, but had a tick in the back of it. It was displeasure.

"No." Bree stood. She looked at him. No. No, what? What was happening? What was she going to do? Her promotion was disappearing. Possibly her job too.

"I thought you were the right person for the opening, but perhaps I was wrong."

She panicked. She stepped forward, into his torso, cupping going on with her hand. "No," she said. Mouth was on its own again. "Anything," she said, quietly.

"Anything," he repeated. His eyes in hers.

He looked almost unsure. Surprised. As she handled his junk. She didn't want to. She felt sick. But she had to. What choice did she have? Eyes in his, the whole time. His cock in her hand, getting it harder in his shitty suit. She couldn't say anything to anyone, could she? He was the boss's son. She *couldn't* just say *no* and *leave*. She'd be fired or moved to some shit position somewhere else, probably before the end of the day. She dropped down him. His perfume stronger at his face, than lower, like getting to the floor for air. Crouching at his waist, pulling open his trousers. Cock coming out. At least it was clean. "Anything," she whispered to herself, before slipping it between her lips.

She felt it flex.

Wanted to puke already. Jesus Christ, what was she doing?

Keeping her job, that was what she was doing.

No. She was giving a blow job to this ... this cunt. For what? Money? This wasn't her. She slipped from him, and looked at the thing, flapping about in front of her face. Fuck. *No*.

"Yes," he said. He put his hand under her arm and pulled her up to stand. Like her doing that had opened some floodgate inside him. He turned her, pushing her face first against the desk. Before she knew what he was doing, his hand had pulled her dress up, hand underneath, on her panties. Pulling at them. Rough. Pulling them down.

"No," she said. She tried to bat his hand away, but he was at an angle. Had her over the desk, pushing her down. She could feel him, probing her pussy, his fingers jabbing at her, inept, careless. "No, I don't want that."

His fingers dug into her hair, and he pushed her face into the food. The smell of it, strong, rank now it was cold. Fatty. Greasy smell. Suddenly the most important smell in the world.

"Liam," she said, louder. "What are you doing?"

He grunted, pulling her panties roughly from her, down, she felt them on her knees.

"*What the fuck*," she screamed. Her hands trying to push her up, and while he wasn't a strong man, he had her down. Weight on her. She'd left it too late to stop him like that. Her hands flailing around behind her. She could feel him pushing at her, his prick looking for her. He was going to fuck her. "No," she screamed. "Help."

"*Help*."

Then he was inside her. She tried to pull, and push, and squirm, but his weight was on her. Holding her down. Fire burnt between her legs. Agony as he pulled at her skin, trying to relieve himself. Leaning further over her, his body on hers, she struggled to get air, as he jerked forward, back. Over and over.

She was crying. Without air. She'd stopped flailing, and twisting, just waiting for it to stop. She whispered some words, begged for him to stop, but it was lost on him. "Yes," he said, "Fuck."

Then it got a little easier. The pain lessening slightly. She thought maybe she'd started bleeding and it was lubing him. Then she realised as he jerked and shuddered, that he'd come in her, and he was just stroking out the last of his seed inside her. Before he stood up. The weight from her, she could breathe again. But he was still there. In her. Getting smaller. Until he slipped out.

She could hear him breathing. Having just come. He stepped back.

Bree stayed there. On the desk. Breathing the stank of the breakfast. That had been a waste of money, too.

"Well," he said. "Get up."

She did. She pushed herself to her feet, and stood there, facing the desk. The wall. Liam still behind her. His seed was slipping down her leg. Drooling from her. Instinctively she wanted to do something. But all she could see were paper serviettes from the bag.

"Get yourself together," he said. He came around the desk, already had his cock away, he was straightening his clothes. He looked her down. "Well?"

Bree didn't know what to do, so she pulled her panties up, his cold sticky cum pulled around as her dress flopped down over herself. She wiped her face with the back of her hand, felt the tears slide, pushed across her face.

"Go and clean up," he barked. He wouldn't look at her.

She burned red. She couldn't think straight, not at all. Nothing. What had just happened? They'd just … had sex. They'd just fucked.

No.

He'd just fucked her.

He was looking at her now. He looked more angry than anything else. Had a look on his face like he was about to start shouting at her.

Bree shook her head. She wanted to say something. Do … something. But all she did was turn and step out of the room. Without word. She even pulled the door carefully closed. Blurting out a sob as soon as he was on the other side of the closed door. She turned and ran towards the lift. Tears flooding her face. Her mind turning around. She got to the lift and pushed the button.

As she stood there in silence, she could hear the faint tap of something dripping to the carpet.

Chapter 9

Raymond had gently awoken Gel when they got home, and as she shuffled off towards the bedroom, Raymond had brought everything in from the car. Started to unpack it all. He was concerned about her habit. It was getting slowly worse, and each time she'd tried to pull it back and reign it in, she'd only gotten back to it even harder.

Everything from barbs and painkillers to coke and ket.

Whatever took her fancy. And, to be honest, he wasn't her keeper. He wasn't even her husband, not legally, anyway. But he wanted her to clean up. Of course he did. He unzipped the bag and started hauling out the laptops and cameras. Only because he didn't want her going anywhere.

Christ. He was going to have to tell her he loved her at some point, wasn't he?

He placed the cameras down on a tray on the table and turned the PC on. Let that boot up for a few minutes while he did this. He put the two laptops on top of each other and took them to the workshop. Down on the counter. Plugged in and opened up. Booted in BIOS. Needed to get the app running to burn a new MAC address into them. If he did that then they were completely untraceable to the last stream, and he could use them again without anyone on the dark web knowing he was re-using hardware.

It wasn't professional, or even savvy, but he had to cut a few corners these days, even with the income becoming healthier with some of these new customers.

His phone buzzed. His brother. Something about his mum needed picking up from the hospital on Thursday. He thought for a second. That should be fine. Said so much in a message and sent it.

Started the app on the laptops.

Back to the living room.

He glanced down at the cameras. Just needed cleaning off. He could do that while he watched TV later. But he was tired. Working all night, then the drive home. It had taken a lot out of him. He slipped into the computer chair and opened the email. Old fashioned he was. Didn't believe in doing it on his phone. Phones were for phone calls, texting, and occasional pictures of Gel doing something cute. His eyes drifted from the screen to the bedroom door. She hadn't closed it, but was fast asleep. He could hear her light snoring. Like a cat snore. More cutesy than annoying. A small smile appeared on his face and he turned back to the email.

There was a message from Luca. Probably not his real name, but Raymond wasn't about to bring that up in polite conversation. He snorted at the message subject. *You owe me rabbits*, it said. Yes. Rabbits. No idea where Luca got his lingo from but Rabbits were money. To be honest, he found using the email to transact all well and good but it was so traceable that he was surprised that Luca hadn't been caught for dealing yet. Fucking coded messages bullshit like they were Russian spies. *Garbage*.

He opened the message and skim read it down. Luca was saying that they owed him five grand on top of the ten. From what Raymond could make of the mess of code it was supposed to be interest. He was pretty sure that Luca was just piling debts up now like it was Jenga, but what are you going to do? This was the reason why you didn't use dealers off the dark web. Christ, if Gel had gone down to a local hoods dealership and was buying everything—even at the inflated prices Luca charged—then he could just go down there and sort him out. You know, the old fashioned way. But she was in far too deep and Raymond had no idea what sort of connections Luca had, and how much they knew about her. Before he'd gotten involved. Before he'd secured her online persona. Made her untraceable, even to those bastards. He glanced again at the open door. Most ordinary men would just tell Luca that all that cash was owed by Gel and hand her over, but Raymond wasn't about to do that. He'd just have to get another job on. Quicker this time. Maybe tonight, even. See if he could drum up enough to wipe the slate clean.

He closed the email.

If he didn't pay it, he dreaded to think what Luca might do to one or both of them.

Pushing himself from the seat, he kicked his shoes off and entered the bedroom. Pulled his shirt off, jeans.

He looked down on Gel, naked, and half-covered by the sheets. She was fucking gorgeous. He was a lucky man. He sat, twisting himself in between the sheets, and as he did, her arm came over him, and she pulled herself to him, half-conscious.

"I love you baby," she muttered from within some drug induced delirium.

"I love you too," he whispered after a pause. He wondered if she would remember the words later. He lay back. Looked at the ceiling. A quick look at the clock. Maybe if he got five hours. He could use the backup shoot location he'd been sitting on. Gel could catfish for a couple of hours while he got the word out that there was going to be a special tonight. Drum up some business. Some of the players that dropped off last night.

Last night's big spenders probably wouldn't return tonight. So he needed whatever the clients that dropped off would want.

He closed his eyes.

Back ached from the drive.

Head ached from the worry. Fuck it. Maybe he should start playing the lottery.

Chapter 10

Mike had ground stare, except it wasn't the ground. It was the keyboard. And it wasn't *his* keyboard, it was the keyboard of the work laptop. He sighed. His thoughts on *his* laptop. Not the work one. A look at the time. It was ready to log on but he still had half an hour. So he turned his chair around to *his* laptop and looked at the video playing. Unsolved mysteries had led him to serial killers had led him to brutal unsolvable crimes and the *new underground*. All night. He thought he'd probably dozed off at one point, because somewhere in the middle of it all, it stopped making sense for a while. But apparently killing these days was big money.

Streamed killings from what some people referred to as *Red Rooms*.

Mike had his doubts that it was real. Which was a shame, because, to be honest, he found it extremely intriguing. But the videos were all blurred and grainy and it just seemed so … *put on*. According to the last video he'd watched the answer all lay on the dark web—which he, again, thought possibly complete bullshit—but they explained it, about how the dark web was just sites that were uncatalogued (lurking, if you will) there, kind of next to the regular internet. Made sense. A specific browser and you could access it. He worked in IT. He could work it out.

And to some extent, he had.

All the regular videos he'd seen had told him not to go to the dark web, because he'd do something stupid, or he'd see something stupid, and he'd get himself killed. Which was just them trying to scare people into not accessing the sites, and seeing that it was all, in actual fact, *bullshit*.

So he had managed to install the *magic* browser, and managed to find his way to the gateway of the dark web. It was all very unimpressive. It looked like a webpage from the late nineties. But there *were* all the things he was told would be there, all the things he was told to stay away from, because he would get killed.

So he started to poke the bear.

See what he could find.

Bree jabbed the key at the lock on her front door. She didn't really remember getting home. She'd driven, but it had all been a bit of a wash. Finally getting the key in, she pushed the door open. In, closed the door behind her. She leant her back against it. Her phone vibrated again. She looked at it. Leslie. Wanted to know where she was. Said her bag was still there, and *where the hell was she, was she okay?*

She thumbed back another message, one that had come in when she was driving, she guessed. Leslie. *Liam looks pissed, why aren't you at your desk?*

Fuck.

She discarded the phone to the table next to the door. Kicked her shoes off, and went to the bedroom, through to the shower. Turned it on. Pulled her clothes off. Got in.

She just stood there.

The burning hot water running down her body. Off. Tears mixing with the water. She grabbed the soap and started cleaning herself. Washing him off her. Over and over. Never not seeing his dirt there. She ended up down on her knees, scrubbing herself, red raw, trying to get this shit from her.

Trying and failing.

Mike had turned on the TV in the living room half of the living room and had it streaming the videos on the regular internet, silently. So they were playing. All the time. He had his headphones and mic on, talking to some jack-off about a monitor that supposedly had turned up with a crack on the screen, even though it had been signed for as received over a week ago, and on his laptop, he was looking at a forum on the alleged dark web, selling illegal drugs.

He'd smoked a joint or two in his time, done a line of speed once, but nothing more really. He was looking to see if he thought any of it looked real. He reckoned he was smart enough to know just by looking. He would be able to tell if it was really people selling drugs or if this whole thing was just some bullshit joke, a scam maybe, to get people like him to buy things with real currency. Take the money and run.

Except it wasn't real money. It was digital money. Which he also hadn't dipped into, really. He had a small stash of something. Couldn't remember what. He'd brought it like it was stock. Just a few quid's worth. See what would happen. Through Paypal if his memory served. He'd have to look into it.

He glanced over to the video on the TV. Blurry bullshit video was actually easier to see when he was all the way across the room from it. Looked like a skin flick with the filter over top, like those pay per view channels on Freeview. But without hearing it, it was impossible to tell.

"So can I send it back?" the douche said.

"Really?" Mike sounded agitated, even to himself. "You really think I'm gonna fall for that?" He'd gone off script. Looked at the screen. He was supposed to have said *yes, of course*, and started taking the guys' details for the return. What did big companies care about someone dropping a monitor and returning it?

"What?" the guy said.

"Fuck," Mike whispered.

"I want to speak to your supervisor."

Mike shook his head. "Go fuck yourself," he snapped. Killed the call. He looked at the screen. Shit. If his manager was watching or listening in …

… You know what? Fuck it. He didn't need this job anyway. He had money in the bank. His old nan had left him a stash months ago, and he still hadn't touched it. If they fucked him off, he'd be okay.

Another call flashed up on the screen to answer, but Mike pulled his headset off and dropped it on the keyboard, his attention turned wholly back to his laptop.

The more he looked at it, the more real it seemed.

Chapter 11

Raymond awoke to Gel stroking his torso, gently. Her body hot, pushed against his. He quickly looked at the time, the first thing he did look at, before turning his attention to her. It was still before lunch. Her kick must have worn off, and she was wide awake. He let out a grunty moan. Only had a few hours of sleep. Wanted more.

He also knew he needed to get up and tell her that they needed to work today. Gently tell her why, too. Without the *Luca is going to fuck us up* parts. Gel's hand went down his body, into his shorts. On his hair. Twisting in it. His cock rolled to the side, gaining enough to move on its own, at which point she grabbed it.

"I see," she whispered. Her lips then taking his nipple, her teeth. A little bite.

His cock grew in her hand. Raymond tried to move but she used her body to gently hold him down. She stroked him slowly. Tongue on his body. Raymond breathing harder. He closed his eyes, but all he saw was that corpse from last night. This morning. Whatever.

"What is it baby?" she said, moaning the words out like a desperate slut. "Come on, daddy," she said.

It wasn't difficult for her to cultivate him through to complete hardness. His cock as big as it could be in her hand now. Her mouth inches from his chest as she spoke, a tiny string of saliva going from her to him. She smiled. Releasing his cock, she slid down his body and took his engorged member in her mouth, sliding down it.

The heat rising in Raymond. "Fuck," he muttered.

She released him from her mouth, and whispered, "Yes, daddy." Climbing naked over him, straddling him. She took his cock in her hand and guided it inside her, all the way down, she sat on him, letting out a little moan of pain, like he was too big for her. All the right moves. She rocked back and forth, her hands plated on his chest, face screwed up like she was caught somewhere between pleasure and pain and she loved it. He moved his hips in time with her gyrations, almost desperate to come. She moved quicker, little sharp cries and grunts like he was the best fucking lover in the world, as he lay there, prone.

"Oh, God," she said.

His cock was flexing. He was close.

"Oh, God, I'm going to come," she said.

Raymond's orgasm burned through his hips, his strokes juddering as he came, Gel almost screaming the house down. "Fucking hell, *yes*." As Raymond slowed, his cock losing girth, she slumped forward, onto his chest, heaving air in and out like she'd just taken the whole England football team. "You're amazing," she whispered.

Raymond couldn't help but grin, and when she looked up at him, she giggled. "What?" she said. She slipped from him, rolling quickly to the side and up, out the bed. "Make me a coffee," she said, sprinting from the room. "Quick shower."

Raymond lay there. Looking at the ceiling. He drew air in and out. Cock still twitching like there was still life left in the old dog yet. He blinked. Saw the corpse in the flash of darkness. Then pushed himself onto his elbows. She was singing. In the bathroom, the power shower was running. Cindy Lauper. He snorted. Pulled his shorts back up, and stood. Legs like jelly. Always was after he'd come. He shook his head, pulled a t-shirt from the drawers and dragged it tightly over his torso. Could feel the cold damp of his cum in his pants. He'd better shower after she did.

Raymond went to the kitchen and flipped the kettle on. He looked at it for a second, then flipped it off. Filled the coffee machine instead. Fancy coffee. She shouted, *wee*, at the top of her voice, and then the shower died. He pulled out the mugs, and sat at the table. Waiting, he pulled his phone and looked at the news. Nothing about them finding a body. He didn't expect there to be anything. Christ, even if someone had found a body this quickly, he doubted that it would be all over the news.

No, it was all the new Prime Minister, the financial crisis. Protesters on the motorway again. He snorted a laugh. At least they hadn't hit that sort of shit on the way home last night.

"Smells good," Gel said, at the door.

Raymond looked from his phone to her. A smile. "I love you."

She crossed the room and pulled herself around his head, hugging it to her breasts, warm, in a dressing gown. "Me too." She released him. "Gonna put on something toasty," she said. "Chilly." She hurried from the room.

Rush, rush, rush, he thought. Oh, to have that energy. Of course, she could have had some speed in the bathroom. He turned and looked at the coffee. Almost done. He carried on with the milk, sugar, as she returned, a small t-shirt, barely covering her waist, and a pair of tight jeans. *Very warm*. She slumped down in the chair.

"So what's on for today?" she said.

He knew she was expecting a lazy day. Nice and easy. Didn't make it any easier. "I got an email from Luca. I want to do another job. As soon as." He turned and put the mugs down, hot coffee stink spilling from them, filling the space.

She shrugged. "Okay. When?"

"Today."

Her face fell. Lip went in between her teeth. "Oh." She took the coffee that he put in front of her. Stared into it.

"You've been hitting it all pretty hard," he continued, trying to be gentle about it. "We owe him. He's demanding more. I just want to pay him off. Maybe find someone new?" Raymond raised his eyebrows, hoping that she was going to respond positively.

"Okay," she said. Eventually looking up to him. "Where, though? Don't we need prep time?"

"I've got a place that I've had up my sleeve for a while, just for an emergency."

"Where?"

"Little place near the city. Farmland. Nice and quiet."

"Damn it," she blurted. *Harsh*. "Fuck. Why? Why now?"

Raymond shrugged. "Doesn't matter. You know what'll happen if we don't choke up the money."

Gel stood up and stalked over to the sink. Poured the last of her coffee down into it. "What do you want me to do?"

Oh so much. Maybe not spend the whole day

sticking shit up your nose? Raymond sighed. He sat back staring at his coffee. Couldn't very well say that now, though, could he? "There isn't a lot you can do. Not yet. Start flipping through the app. See what you can see, but don't start anything. Not until I'm sure we're going where I think."

She nodded. The city. Sure. She looked down at her phone. "No problem."

Chapter 12

Vic stood waiting at the bus stop. There was a woman standing next to him who was really nice. At least, that was his thought. She hadn't spoken. Hadn't so much as looked at him. But he'd caught her perfume between the light wind, and he'd glanced at her, and hell, he'd decided. *She was nice.* The bus was going to be busy and there was only going to be two seats left, next to each other, and he was going to offer her the window seat, and they'd get talking.

His stomach made a light growl. He shouldn't have skipped breakfast. The bus coming, Vic pushed his phone back into his pocket. Pulled out the correct change from his trousers. The change he'd put in there while readying for work that morning. The bus stopped. He thought about letting the woman get on first, but then his gallantry wouldn't play out like it did in his head. He had to get to the empty seats first.

His heart dropped when he got on the bus and there was virtually no one on there. Like most days. He went and sat in the middle. Maybe she'd seen him and would come and sit next to him anyway. Vic pushed himself as close into the window as he could, making as much space as he could and then watched as she went upstairs to the top deck.

He drew in air through clenched teeth, and then turned his attention to the world passing outside the window. Passing the school, he looked at the women dropping their kids off. All getting out of massive motors, some of the mums barely dressed. They had to be cold. His eyes ran down a couple of the girls. Shook his head. No way of knowing how old kids were anymore. Could be eleven, could be sixteen. Christ, he was getting old. But damn it, kids didn't dress like they used to.

He looked at one particularly healthy looking lad. Couldn't be more than fifteen. He had the start of a beard. *A fucking beard.*

The bus turned and suddenly the school, the kids, and the mums were gone. Vic's attention went to the other passengers. On the lower deck, there was a couple of old people. A young bloke. Looked like he had a sinus infection, red nose, like. And that was it. Just them and him. Should have gone and sat upstairs. Like a normal young man.

The bell went and the bus pulled to a stop. A young woman came down. She was wearing a uniform from one of the local supermarkets. Sexy thing, she was. Had a short skirt on. Legs everywhere. Probably cold. But he could warm her up. Vic blinked away the thought and stopped staring at her.

Crikey. The bus, off again, towards the centre. He pulled his phone and looked at the next woman on the app. Shock of red hair. Not naturally red, like Toyah red. From that band. Punk red. Bet her carpet didn't match the curtains. He shook his head, checked the interested box. Like he was ever going to find out. He looked at her other pictures. Never had been one for red hair, but he still would.

The bus pulled in at the centre, and Vic pushed his phone in his pocket, his carrier bag wrapped around his wrist, with his lunch in it, dragging behind him. Everybody got up, and even with little to no people on board, there was plenty of pushing to get off. He nearly pushed the woman from his stop from her feet as she came from the stairs.

"Hey," she said. Gave him a dirty fucking look.

Vic smiled at her. Part apology, part sexy. Neither seemed to work as she pulled away from him out into the throng of people, and disappeared into the crowds of people. Probably never to be seen again.

He climbed down the steps of the bus and hurried along the curb, getting out the way of the people. To the corner and into the pedestrian zone. A bike whapped past him, nearly sending him spinning. Fucker.

Vic went to the door of the estate agent he worked in and tried it. Locked. He banged on the glass and Cathy came over, opening it up. "Running late?" she asked. A smile. Chewing gum. Her eyes in his.

"Yeah," Vic grunted. He went by, leaving her to lock up behind him. "What's on the schedule today?"

She followed him over to the desks, and pulled the bookings from her desk over to his. Slipped it down in front of him, leaning forward, over the desk. She asked if he wanted coffee?

"Cheers," he said, opening the ledger. He could smell her perfume, even after she'd walked away. His finger on the page. "Daniel has a lot on today."

"He does," she said. She brought his coffee without asking how he wanted it. No need. She knew.

Vic looked at the bookings. One day he was going to get a sales job there. Then he was going to earn enough money that he could have any of them.

Whoever he so chose.

Chapter 13

Mike pushed the work laptop to the side. His manager had scheduled a meeting for eleven o'clock. Probably to fire him. He wasn't assigned any calls, so he was supposed to what, just sit there and think about what he'd done?

Well fuck that.

He tossed the headset on the keyboard, and turned his attention back fully to his own laptop. He'd spent half the morning trying to get his head around crypto currency above and beyond what Paypal thought he should buy, and now owned some, which was something. He looked at the sites. Some weird looking menu system, but not what he was led to believe he was going to find on the spoopy dark web. He snorted out a laugh. Something to buy, to see if it was all real.

He navigated his way into a forum, people talking about buying and selling baseball cards. Mike didn't know shit about baseball. He'd seen things on TV. It was like Rounders but huge in the States. Fine. That would do. He tried to hedge into the conversation. Clearly a newb. Everyone talking around him.

He managed to work out that they were trading virtual baseball cards. Some of which were incredibly high value, some very low. He watched two of them talk around some deal. Then they agreed to move to a private room. Then they were gone.

Mike raised an eyebrow. This all seemed like absolute horseshit. He looked at the other people in the room. There were three of them. No one speaking. It was like they were all watching each other suspiciously. Mike typed in, "Anyone want to sell anything, I'm new here."

There was a silence for a moment, and one of the others said, "What you looking to buy?" Their name was Algernon.

"What you got?" Mike replied.

Algernon disconnected.

How rude. Mike looked down the usernames. "Anyone?"

"You don't fit in here."

"Look," Mike replied. "I'm just trying to find my way around. You have cards for sale?" He frowned into the screen. For fuck's sake, he just wanted to buy something. Anything. Something to prove you *could* at least buy something.

"What are you looking for?" Geddy replied.

"Baseball cards." Mike didn't really know what they were asking. He'd already said he was new there.

"Private room?"

"Yes," Mike replied. Hold on, maybe he was getting somewhere. A link popped up on his screen. A link to a private forum room. Mike clicked it. The screen changed, and suddenly he was facing a webcam meeting room. His mic and camera were off, so his window came up black. The other window had the shape of a person in it, but it was shaded and hard to see. Mike squinted into it.

"Turn your fucking shit on, Mike," Geddy said. "Fucking muppet."

Mike blinked at the laptop screen for a second,

before fumbling to turn on the mic and camera. "How did you know my name?"

Geddy snorted. He read Mike's address out to him.

Mike just watched. Stared. He'd seen online about how they could find you on the dark web and shit like that, but ... *fucking hell*. This guy knew his name and where he lived in an instant. "Wow," he said.

"So, Mike," Geddy said, reinforcing that he knew the information. "Tell me what you're looking for."

Mike swallowed. He was in deeper than he was expecting, but he didn't dislike the feeling. "What do you look like?" he asked, unable to see much of the man he was dealing with.

"You really are new at this, aren't you? Look. I'm gonna cut you a break. Don't ask people on here who they are. I mean, what the fuck, I can see you clear as day, and you have no idea what you're doing. I could be the cops, man." He stayed back in the shadows. "You have money?"

Mike nodded. "What can I get?"

"Fuck," Geddy breathed. "Jesus man. I have Babe Ruth, you want Babe Ruth? It's a starter card."

"How much?"

"You have to ask, you can't afford, am I right?"

Geddy had an accent that Mike couldn't quite put his finger on. It wasn't American. Not British. Not quite Australian. "Okay," he said. "How do I?"

Another link appeared in the window. "Click the link, and the money comes straight from your wallet, then I transfer the card."

"How do I know I can trust you?"

Geddy started laughing. "Fucking hell, man. You think I'm a cunt? You know a cunt would rip you off.

Do I look like a cunt?"

Mike couldn't tell if Geddy looked like a cunt or not, because he couldn't see him. "No, of course not." He clicked the link, his cursor spun for a second and then the transaction was apparently complete.

Then another link appeared.

"You click that one for your card."

Mike could see Geddy shaking his head.

"Good luck Mike. Try not to get yourself killed."

Then Geddy was gone. Mike stared at the link. Okay. So he'd just completed a transaction on the dark web with a man called Geddy for a Babe Ruth starter card. That cost him some money. He had no idea how much. Mike had transferred one hundred pounds to his crypto wallet. He opened a different browser window and checked. Babe Ruth had cost him fifty fucking pounds. A starter card. Mike scowled at the link. He wanted to slam the fucking laptop shut. Bastard had fucking ripped him off. Fucking fifty quid for a fucking link to a fucking virtual card. He sucked air in. Cunt.

Mike looked at his phone. He still hadn't heard from fucking Bree.

His attention went back to the link. Right. Play fair. Click on the link. Get the fucking card. At least have something to show for it. It had better not have a virus. He shook his head. No. Trust in the weirdos on the web. Trust in them.

He held his breath and clicked on the link.

The screen changed and the card opened. A picture. The card. Not the Babe Ruth he was expecting. Sure, he had no fucking idea what Babe Ruth looked like, but this wasn't it. The picture was of a young girl. Maybe four. She was clothed, decently, but staring at the camera. She looked like

she'd seen some shit. Haunted. Horrified.
   Terrified.

CHAPTER 14

Bree stared into the middle of nothing, looking at her memories, wondering if she could have done something differently. Of course, she could have done something differently. There had to have been something that would have stopped this from playing out the way that it did. Right?

Right?

She looked at the phone, sitting on the floor in front of her. It had buzzed again, vibrating against the cold tiles only a few minutes ago. Probably Leslie. She'd wanted to know why Bree had disappeared. Left her bag. Not been at work. Not come back. Should she call someone?

No. Bree still looked at the phone. Perhaps she should though. But who? Who could she talk to that might understand? There was Mike. He was the first person who came to mind, but he was the last person she wanted to talk to. He'd flip out. Belt fast off the deep end, and want to go to the office and prove himself a man by twatting Liam. Only problem was that he'd probably lose the fight. Once he'd gotten into this half barney in the pub, and she thought he was really going to fuck the guy up, but when push came to shove he backed down, siting that he didn't want to get barred. And of course, he'd want a reward for being the good guy.

Bree pulled the blanket she had wrapped around

her closer. The knit on it tickling her bare skin. Red. Raw.

Her mum. She would apply the right amount of caring, but fuck it would she want her to call the police. Tell them he'd raped her. But he hadn't, had he? She closed her eyes, hating herself for even considering pleasing him in that way. She should have just got up and slapped him. Or told him she could climb the fucking ladder the right way. But she hadn't. And look at what it had got her.

And he was probably putting together her papers now, firing her for walking out.

Probably had a report all written out that she instigated it all.

A tear rolled quickly down her face.

She'd fucked this all up. Just by being stupid. She straightened her legs, the backs of them pushing down on the bathroom tiles, cold and hard. Sniffing up snot back into her throat and swallowing it. Cold. She pushed herself up to her feet. Left her phone where it was. Maybe it was better if she didn't speak to anyone at all. She padded barefoot to the carpet. The warmth of that, a relief, before she continued through to the living room, flopping on the sofa and staring at the wall.

Maybe decorate.

The noise of her phone vibing in the bathroom chattering like teeth on the tiles cutting through the silence. She lay back, rolling down on the sofa and continuing to stare at the nothing.

Chapter 15

Raymond flicked keys on the laptop, putting in the commands half-hearted. Didn't want to do it tonight. He was tired. Time was running on and Gel still hadn't gotten her shit together. He looked at the time. Put the post up.

The clock started.

They now had seven hours give or take to get the meat. Get to the studio. Set up. And start filming.

He could play an hour either way. That wasn't a problem. If he was much more than an hour late, especially if he hadn't started a feed, then he would start to lose clients. Dropping off. They understood why. Shit happened. But it was bad business to tell everyone there was a show, and then not actually have it. Too much of that and people stopped showing up at all. He glanced over to Gel. "You ready?"

She was pushing her uniform into the bag roughly. "I've only just got this out the drier." She looked at him for something.

Sympathy? What? It wasn't like this was his fault, was it? He shrugged. "Just toss it on those." He indicated the bags with the rest of the electrical equipment in them. "Have you found some meat yet?"

She sighed theatrically. "Give me a chance."

Raymond looked from her to the screen. Looked at his phone. His watch. Got the time straight in his head, then closed the laptop. Pulled the cable, and curled it quickly on top.

"You sure this place you've eyed is cool?"

He grunted, nodded. He was. Sort of. He'd been watching it on and off for a while. It should be fine. It was certainly far enough out of town. Looked like it had been a spot for gangs or something in the past, but dead now.

"Electric?" she said.

"No idea." The gen was in the back of the car. They hadn't needed it for several shows now. Which was good. The fucking thing was heavy, and loud. Had to rig it up away from the shoot. Which only made them more obvious. Chugging generators in one part of a building. Screaming torture in another. He placed his bag on top of the others. "You gonna find the meat while I drive, then?"

"Yes," she hissed. "Fuck."

Mike had looked at the phone long and hard while deciding what to do with it. It was clearly some gateway child porn shit. Babe Ruth. Not what he was there for. That was the last thing. Equally, though, it wasn't actual kiddie shit, so there was no reason not to keep it. It wasn't like he was doing anything wrong.

So he kept it. Stored on the hard drive.

He'd decided to decide what to do with it later. When he knew if there was actually a point to having it or not.

He sloped from forum to forum. People talking about all sorts. Most of it was banal bullshit—nothing you wouldn't see on any social media. Which was weird. He sat back, beer in hand, his thumb rolling around the lip of the bottle. What had he been expecting? Gangsters sitting at virtual tables. Pictures of piles of drugs. Guns. Apparently child porn? Seemed to be the easiest thing to find. At least, so *he'd* found. He shook his head. Scrolled down this forum. There was a guy touting hitman services and everyone was ignoring him like he was some leper or something.

Probably just as new as Mike.

He continued down the forum, found himself in some movie section. People talking about banned films. Films that supposedly had real snuff in them. One of these losers was saying something about American Guinea Pig, and even Mike had seen some of that. It was about as real as Two and Half Men. A couple of the others were taking the piss out of him.

Mike looked at the usernames. No idea why he just assumed they were all blokes. Their usernames were all gender neutral, for lack of a better term. One of them was called Teapot. He looked at his own username. Computer generated number sequence. Random, he guessed. Shit. That probably gave him away as a newb to anyone who knew. He jumped into his profile and highlighted the number sequence. Fuck. What should he call himself? He needed a name that was cool, but also … hard. Like he was a gangster, and he shouldn't be messed with. He thought long and hard, and settled on Baller. That would do.

He closed the window and the name updated. Then he told Teapot that he was a weirdo and there weren't any real snuff films. Certainly nothing he'd heard of, anyway.

Teapot stopped what he was doing, eventually replying, "What do you know, Baller?"

"I know what I've seen. I know that there isn't

any real shit like that, and this place is bullshit."

Raymond started the car. He glanced over to Gel. "Hold up?"

She looked over to him. "I just need to set up the profile. Where are we going to pick up?"

"North of the city. There's a club district there. Try somewhere around there." He pulled out into the traffic and headed towards the ring road.

"Got it." She put the postcode into her phone. Saved it. She looked out the window. Spots of rain on the glass. "Great," she whispered. Her phone immediately started to vibrate. Notifications that people were interested in her. She smiled. She was using real body shots to get the boy's attention. The only fakes were the face shots. Just so she couldn't be identified by the police later. She looked at the arse shot in the private section. Two people had already hearted it, and she had three people looking to meet up. "It's always so much easier to pick up a boy," she said. She pointed the phone at Raymond, but he didn't look at it. Focussed on the traffic. "What sort of boy would you like?"

"Someone different."

Vic left work and trotted straight to the bus stop. The weather was coming over and he really didn't want to get wet. In fact all he wanted to do was get home and change out of this fucking suit. He hated having to go into the office, especially when he was nothing more than a glorified receptionist. Half the time these days everybody booked shit themselves online and there was no need for either him nor Cathy. But they had rules and rules were meant to be followed.

He pulled his phone and looked at the time. Shit.

He must have been a few minutes late getting out of the office. He just missed the bus. Have to wait for the next. He walked back over to the wall, away from the madding crowd and leaned there. Opened his dating app and looked at the latest in a line of hot young women who would ignore him completely, or worse, block him.

He looked at the newest listed. See if he couldn't strike while the iron was hot. A young girl. Mousy looking librarian type. He looked at her chest. Couldn't tell much from the angle of the shot. Checked the interested box. Swiped to the next. Woman in a swimsuit. Checked. Next. Woman with blond hair. Just a head shot. Pretty girl. He thumbed down into her profile and looked at her other pictures. She had a body and wasn't afraid to show it. She had nice cleavage and a cute bum. He looked at the time on the profile. Just created, updated a couple of minutes ago. And her postcode was local to him. He looked at her wants. She loved brains. Muscles a turn off. Nice guys only. Nerds need apply.

Nerds need apply.

He looked down himself. Holy shit. He was a nerd. A nice guy. And he didn't have muscles. His finger over the check box. He was interested, but something stopped him. Something from back at school. The girls that teased him. Led him on. Said they liked him. Before he was dragged out in front of everyone, laughing at him. He closed his eyes and waited for his confidence to return. That was a long time ago. Times were different. He was different. He wasn't that fucking loser anymore. But he did meet her requirements. He checked the box. Interested.

What was the worst thing that could happen?

Mike said, "You can't see me shrug, but I'm shrugging." All those fucking Youtube videos were bullshit. There was no darkness down here, apart from a few fucking weirdos with creepy photos of kids. The dark web. Pfft.

Oberon replied. "Okay then."

A link popped up on Mike's screen. He looked at it. He was doubtful. He'd been here long enough to know that everything he'd encountered was just bull. Even that fucking photo that had gotten him a little twisted. It was probably just a still from a movie or something. Something harmless.

So he clicked on the link. Just to see what he would get from this. Obviously, it was going to be nothing.

The link opened a new window.

It was a show. There was a timer running down. Long fucking wait. Like hours. He snorted his abject dissatisfaction at the idea that he was going to have to wait five fucking hours to see what? At best, it was going to be some lame-arse peep show, one that probably didn't have any real pussy in it, or, somewhat more likely in his opinion, it was going to be some crapshoot magic show, where someone got *sawn in half.* Oh, the *oo*'s. The *ar*'s. He looked around the edge of the screen. There was a link to a chat room. That was probably full of tossers and edgelords too. But he still clicked on it.

Somewhere in the back of his mind, there was definitely some intrigue. But it was fucking waning. Oh how was it. The link took him through to a green room.

Oberon said, "Took you time."

Mike shook his head. "What of it? I mean, I'm not hanging around for five hours for a fucking peep show."

"Your loss," said Parker. Whoever he was. "Best show in town this one. Still. You want to give up your seat, then I'm sure there'll be a queue in a couple of hours of people waiting to take it."

Mike had his fingers poised over the keyboard and mouse. He was ready to call it. Uninstall all this bullshit and see if he could get hold of Bree. Maybe get her over to fuck. But there was something about the way they didn't care if he stayed or not. So he asked, "What happens in the show?"

The question hung there for a moment, like everyone in the room was either trying to think of an answer, or, how to berate him for being so innocent. He wished he hadn't asked. Okay, his interest was piqued now. The suggestion laying there, that he couldn't leave the room and maybe come back later. Which in equal parts loaded up on the intrigue and pissed him off at the same time. "I think I'll hang around," he said. "See how this plays out."

"Can I offer you anything while you wait?"

Mike looked at the offer. It was from Room101. He honestly wondered what would happen if he asked for something. "What do you have?"

"Hold on," 101 said.

Mike just watched the cursor blinking.

"I see where you are. I can have coke, meth, or E to you in thirty minutes or less. Free if it's longer."

Mike stared at it. What the fuck? He really wanted to find out. Find out what happened if he called them. *Yeah, send me some E.* Problem was, they'd want some of his coin, and he didn't want to get thrown out of this place, not before *knowing*.

"I think our friend here is reticent." Oberon's cursor blinked silently at the end of the line.

Mike was about to say something rash. Something even he didn't know what it was going to be, but certainly something about ordering door to door drugs, when Parker said, "You here last night?"

Oberon replied. "Yeah. Didn't like the show. Wasn't my bag."

"Dino got barred."

"Doesn't surprise me."

Mike sat back and looked at the conversation. Seems they'd forgotten all about him. Fine. He could call them on their shenanigans later.

Raymond pulled the car to the grass, and quickly got out. He looked over the roof to the building. Listening. Nothing but the wind. He slipped back in behind the wheel.

"Nothing?" Gel asked.

"Nope." He started the engine and drew the car over to the side of the building. "You found anyone?"

"Got a couple of possibles." She lifted her arse and pulled down her jeans.

"What the fuck?" Raymond nearly swerved. "Are you fucking ..." Incomplete questions abounded.

She giggled. "Look, if it's someone different you want, then I have to play a different game. Fucking players will hook up with you on demand—these quiet motherfuckers don't trust you." She stuck two fingers crossed in front of her mound and took a photo of it with her phone. Pulled it into a DM and sent it.

"Fucking hell," Raymond muttered pulling up on the door. "I'd better work."

"You ever known me not to pull?" She giggled, pushing herself over the gearstick and almost into his lap, kissing him hard.

Raymond stopped the car. Kissed her back. "Never," he said through heavy breaths. "Never."

She smiled at him, clambered back to her side of the car, and out. To the boot. Stuff pulled out, lugging it into the building, while Raymond quickly scouted the edge of the property and then the inside.

He joined her as she rested the last of the bags down inside the door. "No one for a long time," he said. Had a little smile. Projecting confidence. He wasn't confident. He was relieved. He needed a little luck for this to go off. And that was the first bit. "Make the meet."

Gel nodded. She went back and sat in the car. Door pushed open, feet out through the window. She opened the chat back up.

Vic looked at the picture of her pussy. Fingers there, as he'd suggested. It was real. This chick had sent him nudes. Fucking hell. His cock was already hard. As he sat there, in the window at Starbucks. Fucking hell. The same two words floating about above his head. Was he getting laid tonight?

He was, wasn't he?

He knocked back the last of his hippy chai fuck whatever, and pushed his phone in his pocket. Waited a minute for the risen tide to go down, and then did that little dance all men do when standing up and rearranging the junk. A quick glance. Middle-aged woman sitting a couple of seats down had looked above the top of her Kindle and was staring at him.

Vic gave her a little smile. Flashed it, before turning, smiling properly to himself, and heading down the shop to the door.

Out into the street, and turned in the direction of home.

He needed to change. Shower. Obviously. Should he warm up? You know. He wasn't good at … *that*. Not much practice. If any.

Fuck.

Raymond loaded the cameras into the software, one at a time, checking the angle. Gel was pushing the table back and forth, a little this way, and little that. "It's fine," he said, wishing she would stop the grinding sound of the table leg on the floor every five minutes.

She huffed at him, and then pulled the straps from the holdall at her feet. Opened the packaging. Brand new ones. Same every time. They always stayed with the meat after the show. No sense in getting caught with evidence. She attached them to the table. Expertly. She'd done it before. Once or twice. She whistled a low tune while she worked.

The table was on the next floor up. Raymond had dragged it down the stairs, careful not to break the legs of the thing off. Then he'd found a chair on that floor. He had the laptop he was working on, on the chair, and he was sitting on the floor. "What time you meeting?"

Gel slipped her phone from her pocket. "Couple of hours."

Mike looked from the porn on the TV to the green room. Oberon had told him that once the show was ready to air, then they'd go back to the main room and no longer be able to communicate with anyone, except the Red Room team. Then he'd stopped talking, although he was still in the room. Mike thought that he had probably fucked off somewhere else, and he just left himself logged in this *green room*, to ensure his space was kept.

Mike glanced at the man with the huge cock getting sucked by a *t-boy* on the TV.

Hand on the front of his jeans. He could feel himself.

Vic ran his fingers through his hair, looking at his body in the mirror. It was not a good body. She wasn't going to like it. She was going to laugh at him. And make fun. Probably post it everywhere online.

Fucking hell. Maybe he shouldn't go? He sucked in his little pot and looked at his willy. Hm. This wasn't a good idea.

Then his phone buzzed, and he looked at it. It was hanging out of his trousers strewn across the bathroom floor. Bent naked and picked it up. He looked at it. Message from her. He opened it. It said, "So looking forward to it."

He nodded. So was he. Rather too much. He still wondered if he shouldn't … you know. So he was longer lasting … with her. "Me too," he replied.

But also he didn't want to dribble having used it all up. Oh fucking hell. Why was this shit so complicated? He looked at himself again. Like a fire hose, but maybe quickly? Or longer lasting but maybe a dribble? Fuck. He sighed, and stamped off towards the bedroom, Googling it.

Raymond was tapping his fingers on the steering wheel. He kept looking to the door into the building, waiting for Gel to appear.

"Come on," he muttered under his breath. "Come *on*." He looked at his watch. They had plenty of time. Plenty of it. But he wanted to get out and get back. This bit was the hardest bit, as far as he was concerned, anyway.

Gel opened the door. She was wiping her face with the back of her hand. He watched her walk around the car and get in the passenger seat.

"What have you done?" he asked, very matter-of-factly.

"Line of speed," she said. "Just to get me in the mood."

Raymond scratched the top of his forehead. He was sure it was higher than it was a while ago. Maybe he was losing his hair? "Right," he said. Starting the engine.

"Right," Vic said. He decided to go for *a lot, and maybe quick*, on the off chance that he could go twice. Big ask, but he'd done it ... himself ... before now. He closed the door behind him, and started to hoof to the north end of the town. That was where the clubs were and she was going to meet him up there. She said she wanted to meet to the side of Flingo. Which was a stupid name for a club. It was the one nearest the dual carriageway. Furthest for him to get to, but that meant they had a nice long walk back to his, get to know each other. You know.

Before the gushening.

Chapter 16

Mike,

Shit. I don't even know how to start this. I've got to get away from it all. I don't know. I don't know what I should tell you or how. Fuck. I thought it would be easier doing this over the email.

You just always seem to be looking out for yourself and I don't want that anymore. I thought we might have had something, but you couldn't get your shit together. I started this telling myself that I was just going to go down the 'it's not you, me road', but you know what? You need to hear a few things. You're probably going to get hooked up with some other girl soon enough, and you need to treat her better.

Your flat fucking smells. You smell half the time. All you want to do is fuck and sleep and watch TV and play video games.

No girl is going to want you like that.

Clean your goddamn finger nails, just once in a while.

I've got shit coming down on me left and right, and I don't need to be looking after a man-child like you, as well.

Don't try to contact me.

B

Chapter 17

Vic tapped his foot on the ground. There was a lot of *nightlife* going on outside the front of the club. He was feeling extremely self-conscious, and hating every second of his life. He'd been standing there alone for some thirty minutes now. Granted, he was rather early, but better early than late, as his old mum used to say.

He kept getting looks from the other girls going into the club. Didn't help that he was staring at half of them trying to work out if it was his date or not. Probably looked like a right creeper.

He was keeping his doubt just about at bay. He was sure that she wasn't coming, but hadn't given up. Not yet. Well, maybe a little bit given up.

What was he doing? Picking up fucking girls in the middle of the night outside a club. Then he thought about her pussy photo again, and calmed. A little. Another look around. She wasn't coming, was she? Probably sitting in a car over the road, filming him for some fucking Instagram channel. Japes on You.

He looked back, the direction out of town. It was quieter that way. He could walk back home the long way. The quiet way.

"Hey."

Vic's heart leapt up and took residence in his throat, even before he'd turned and looked. The voice was sweet, and it stirred him. He swallowed back saliva, suddenly drier than the Sahara desert, before he looked up to her. She was standing with the club behind her. The lights of the street causing an iridescent glow around her person, her body. He couldn't help but look down it. She was wearing a short skirt. Tight top. He tried to take in as much as he could, before she realised he was, well, *him*, and changed her mind. He looked at her face. She was smiling, a small, crooked little smile. She didn't look the same as the photos. She was blonder. Maybe that was the light? He was too far back to really take in her features, but he wanted to stay a little back and just admire her. Standing there in the night. "Hey," he said back, after far too much time had gone. Then he couldn't remember her name. Or his, come to that. Fucking hell.

"Vic?" she said.

She had to know. What other pathetic dork was going to be standing there in the middle of the fucking night like a complete—hold on. He stepped towards her. "Yes," he said. Tried to smile. Normal smile. No creepy smiles. She stepped into him, meeting him halfway, her lips straight up into his. Vic felt light headed. This had never happened before. She pulled back, her eyes in his. They were warm. Almost ... loving. He knew how fucking stupid that sounded, but she had this ... *thing* about her. She didn't really look much like her pictures on the app, but what with filters and such, did anyone? Christ, he didn't even know. This was the first proper meet he'd managed to get. They usually bailed on him long before now. He realised her hand was in his. Warming his cold skin.

"Come on," she said. "Why don't we blow the

club and go back to mine. Watch Netflix." She was already stepping away, her hand in his.

What. Was. Happening? Vic smiled. He felt like he was going to either pass out, or puke. Doing both wasn't off the table. He looked at their hands. Like they were a couple. Was this how *hooking up* worked? Shit. He was hooking up with a fine-arse fucking girl. Going back to her place. To watch *Netflix*. And we all knew what that meant.

Vic was hoping it meant what he thought it meant.

She dragged him along and he met the eyes of some of the people outside the club. *Why, yes. She is hot, isn't she? Yes. Taking me home. Uh huh. Netflix*.

And chill.

"Mine's close," she said. "I like your jeans." She looked absently behind her, checking the road, Vic assumed, before pulling him across to the other side like a chicken. "I hope you like me," she continued.

Vic wasn't really saying much. He was concerned about how little blood he had coursing through his body, and whether he was even going to make it back to her place before he … got too excited. "Of course," he mumbled. And he meant it. Fucking hell. She was every fantasy come true. She was a little shorter than him, but he was what other people had called *a long streak of piss*. She had breasts. Like there. Legs. He could see skin. She pulled him around a corner.

He was trying not to look like he was about to pass out. Breathing hard like someone trying to pretend they hadn't had too much to drink.

He looked down the alleyway they were in. Tall buildings on both sides. He'd never been in this alley before. Wondered if she was about to drag him into one of the doors to the flats, or out the other end, when something stung him.

"Ouch," he said, slamming his hand up to his neck. "What the fuck." He tried to pull his hand away from hers. So he could … see. Maybe it was a spider? Too latr in year tp be bwphf wasp …

Vic turned. There was a shadow behind him.

Woh thr fck w …

The world started to turn. He was free of the girl now. The alleyway spinning in the dark. A roller coaster corkscrewing into a tunnel, the lights dimming. Just trying to scare the punters. But the coaster was perfectly safe.

You always came out the other side.

Raymond pulled the boot of the car open. Took the lump of flesh under the arms and pulled. Gel stood watching. Not even offering to help. Grunting for effect. The meat wasn't heavy, not particularly, but she could offer. It wasn't like they were doing this for *his* health, was it? He pulled the meat out the car, its heels dropping down onto the dirt, and Raymond pulled. Taking it to the doors, into the building.

Gel flashing a torch around for a bit of light before they were inside, and turning the lights on that they'd brought with them.

The rooms illuminated, Raymond dropped the meat to the floor. Looked down at him. "Streak of piss," he said, quietly.

"Nice boy though."

"Certainly had eyes for you."

"Don't they always?" She looked up at him and giggled. "How do you want him on the table to start?"

"Let's do it the eighties way."

Gel nodded. Saluted.

A message popped up in the green room. Mike looked at it. Said the event timer was about to start. "What the hell does that mean?"

Oberon replied, "Into the Red Room. That's where you stay. Leave the Red Room now and you can't get back in. No more newcomers. That sort of thing. See you on the other side."

Raymond got the cameras on, and made sure the focus was all on the meat. Bound down, naked to the table. Rather surprisingly the meat had a larger penis. He wasn't expecting that. He was expecting nerd south central. He looked at the picture-in-pictures of the clients on the screen in front of him. "Oberon," he said. "More light."

Oberon moved in, looked into the camera and winked. He had been in enough of these shows, run by what he thought were the same people to know the rules. Just darker on his side than he expected.

"Baller," he said. "No camera, no show."

Baller turned his camera on after a moment. It had taken a few seconds longer than Raymond was happy with. But when he did he just seemed to be a normal looking cunt with a living room in the background. He eyed the background, checking for signs of something out of the ordinary.

Holy shit. Mike looked at the screen. There was a guy on the table. He was breathing slowly. He wasn't expecting it to look this authentic. Not at all. Then the camera changed. One at the guy's feet, higher, looking down on the body. Pretending to be out. Fully naked. Full frontal. At least they were making the effort. He smiled to himself. Suddenly a message popped up. "Baller," it said. "No camera, no show."

Mike stared at it for a moment. What? They would boot him if he didn't have a camera on? Hm. Didn't seem right. Why the fuck did they need to see him? He had his fingers over the keyboard, ready to tell the fucker to go fuck himself ... but he waited. If there was going to be a show, and it was going to be nothing more than a magic show, what harm could it be if they saw his face? Not like you can blackmail someone for watching what was tantamount to being sideshow trickery. If it even got that far.

He took the mouse and switched on the camera. Smiled into it. Wondered briefly who he was smiling at. Then his eyes went back to the screen, the image from the camera.

Gel strode across the room to the meat. She had dressed for the occasion. Her uniform wasn't particularly well ironed, or anything like that, but it would look fine for the camera. The eyes would mostly be on her, after all. Had a whip in her hand. Sex whip. Nothing that would break the skin or anything. You don't want to damage the meat before the show starts, after all. She dangled the thing over the meat. Over his body, running it up his skin. Over his cock. She turned, eye fucked the camera before walking off the set.

Raymond smiled at her. "Nice," he said.

She shot him a wink, leaving out to the next room. She quickly took a swig of the water they'd brought with them. Came back through the other door, out to where Raymond was. She looked down at the screen.

"Lose many?" she asked, a quick glance to the meat. Sometimes the audience preferred a man, sometimes a woman. Bit of girl on girl. But it was always different.

Raymond poked at the screen. "Three or four newbs." He looked at the bloke to girl ratio. "More chicks than usual."

"Here for the meat," Gel said. She waved the sex whip in its direction.

"Got a couple of high rollers I've seen before."

"Should make?"

Raymond dropped his head to the side. "Might. Fingers crossed. Should take twenty." he sighed, "*Better* make twenty."

Gel rested her hand on his shoulder. "It's gonna be okay Baby."

He rested his face down on her hand. Yeah. It was gonna be fine.

She wiggled. "He's waking up by the look of it."

Raymond straightened himself. "Show time."

N O W   S T R E A M I N G

Vic stirred like he'd been out drinking fucking heavily the night before. "Jesus," he muttered. He tried to open his eyes, head thumping from some sorta dehydration. The burn of yellow electric lights passing through the small gap between his eyelids, as he pushed them closed again, failing to get them properly opened. Didn't remember much. Fuck. Yeah. He'd picked up a girl. Outside the club. Going back to her place to fuck.

Did they fuck?

He didn't remember fucking. Fuck. What the hell had happened? Why was he so cold?

Raymond snorted. "One of them wants you to fuck him."

Gel shook her head, oozing onto camera. "That'll cost," she said. She went over to the meat and ran her fingers down his bare chest. The skin on skin sensation, the warmth of her flesh on his. The meat opened his eyes. Bleary. Tired. Looked like he was just slipping out of a coma. He smiled, slowly, looking at her, like his memories were all returning. She crawled up on the table, over him. Her knees one each side of his hips, she gyrated her body down towards him, not quite touching. Her eyes in his. She smiled. Bit her lip. "Good evening," she whispered, far too quiet for the mic's to pick up.

"Hey," he whispered back. His eyes circling her face. Taking her in. "What's up?"

She looked down between them. "You are, by the looks of it." She smiled up into his face. Then she crawled off the table.

The meat looked around, seeing the place for the first time. His cock lolling over his stomach, fatter, excited, but already on the retreat.

Gel looked into the camera. "You need to put your money where your mouth is, if you want me to fuck that," she barked into the camera. Leaning forward. Shot down her top. She'd never put on a fuck show for the cameras before, but it wasn't off the table, not at the right price.

"What the hell?" Vic cried. "What the shit."

Gel turned and looked at him. Grinning. "Hey big boy," she said. She wandered to him, admiring his cock. "I did not expect you to be packing down there."

"What the fuck is this …" his eyes darted around the room, looking for answers, "… fucking sex tape thing?"

Gel started laughing.

Raymond maintained his cool on the side. His eyes continually riding around the screens, checking.

Working.

Mike looked at the guy's cock with a frown. If he'd wanted porn he could have gotten it anywhere. Certainly without this deep dive shit into … *whatever this was*. Fuck it. He was twirling his mouse around the screen. Absently.

Then a message came up. *Show his flesh.*

Mike squinted at it. What the fuck was that supposed to mean?

"Take some skin off," Raymond called, quietly, over to Gel. "It's only five hundred."

Gel was still looking at the meat, the instruction raised her smile to a grin. "No problem," she whispered, never taking her eyes from the meat. She still had the whip in her hand, after all. "You know," she whispered, "I would have liked to have met *that* in a different situation." Her eyes flicking to his flaccid penis. "I bet you come quick, don't you?" she continued. "Gallons." She licked her lips and raised the whip. Sex whip or not—it worked if you hit *hard*.

Vic looked at the crazy bitch holding the whip. She was making a pass at him. Saying something about his cock. He looked at the camera over him, at his feet. Then a look by her to the man sitting in the corner. He seemed really fucking busy with something. Probably editing this shit. Eyes back on the girl. What the fuck was her name? God. If they wanted him in their fuck film they only need to ask. He looked her down. She was in some Nazi getup. A fucking sex costume. Like they were filming a bondage prison movie. He brought air in. This was weird and fucking scary.

She brought the whip up. It was a sex whip, he was saying to himself, in his head. Just a sex whip.

Then she snapped the thing down, her arm a blur. She'd done it before.

The strands of leather or whatever it was flicked across his torso. His body snapped cold. Not so bad. Was a sex whip, clearly. Then the cold subsided to hot, and his nerve endings kicked in and the pain crept out from the source. "Oh, Jesus," he said. He looked down at the red marks across his stomach.

"Fucking hell." The burning increasing in temperature. She brought her hand back again, the whip up. "No," Vic said, "No, what are you doing?"

She snapped it down again, the fire blossoming under his skin. Acid in his flesh. Burning violent heat.

Gel brought the whip up a third time. Third time's a charm, after all. She snapped her arm down. It was all in the elbow. And the whip slashed across his skin. Breaking it open, tiny cuts like paper cuts, abrasions, flecks of coppery blood on his pale white skin. Never seen a day on the beach, this one. She smiled down at him as the pain of the third slash reached his brain and he screamed.

"Please fucking God, what are you doing?"

She raised the whip, again. Down. Up. Down again, before he realised that was five. The blood leached from his wounds, rising as welts on the skin, pulling, and tightening, as his flesh grew, angry and red. She reached forward, slipping her bare fingers into his blood and pushing it about on his body like lotion. "How you doing, lover?" she asked.

The meat made this guttural cry. A grunt like an animal. His eyes staring into hers. Wild and hurt.

She turned back to the camera and went to the one near Raymond. "Now that makes *me* hard," she said, staring into the lens. She turned, faced the meat, and bent over, her fingers toying with her panties, upskirt for the audience. "Oh," she moaned out, faking sexual rise, "*yes.*"

Mike looked at the guy's skin, peeling back like chicken skin under a blow torch, trying to crawl away from the wounds that the girl had made with the whip. This had to be pre-recorded, then. There was no way that these effects could be made on a live stream. Not in real time. This would need all sorts of unreliable prosthetics. He screwed his nose up. But how to prove it? He was in the room, along with a few others, being duped. The instruction that came up on screen was a plant. That would explain why none of them were allowed to leave the room, or talk to each other, or even see each other. So he had to prove it, by demanding they do something to the guy. That they would refuse. Then he'd know.

His fingers hovered over the keyboard. What to ask for? And how much? Shit he didn't have much in his wallet. Fifty, right? Shit. He grinned. He opened a different browser and quickly started to transfer more money. He was going to prove it, once and for all, that this was fucking bullshit.

"One thousand to take a finger."

"Wow," Gel raised her eyebrows, ensuring she did so off camera. She went to the side of the table and grabbed the shears. She gave the meat a quick glance. He was in that place, where he was realising this wasn't a game and he was in a whole shit pile of trouble. His head was to the side. Looking away from them and the cameras, facing the wall. His stomach, glistening with body fluids, was bouncing up and down as he cried. He was muttering and mumbling out some words.

She couldn't hear what they were, but she knew regardless.

He was pleading for her to let him go. Saying he wouldn't say anything. And that they could trust him.

She held his hand down flat. He lurched, the surprise of the human touch, but he didn't resist. That fight was passive for now, for a few minutes. Until after the next thing. She took the shears and slipped them each side of his forefinger. Made sure she was out of the way of the camera. Even gave it a little wink, and then she snapped the shears closed. Butcher's bone shears, designed to go through the flesh and bone with ease, his finger popped off, like a champagne cork and dropped to the concrete floor. A splop.

It took the meat a second or two to realise what had happened and then it started to scream vile blasphemy out at her. He cried, and spat, and squirmed. Before he slowed and stopped, barely able to move. And only making a better show for the camera.

"Next?" she said. She walked back to the camera and addressed the audience. "Now that was hot." She licked her lips and bit at them. The audience cutting from a view of her to that of the meat.

"Newbie Baller, wants you to take his eye for a hundred."

She laughed. "You can do better than that," she said into the camera, while Raymond typed a message, straight to Mike. "Eye's cost more."

Mike looked at the message. Of course they do. *So much that I can't afford it*. That's the game. "A thousand."

Hit send.

Gel took the meat skewer from the kit and the blowtorch, and went and stood over the meat. Showed him both items.

"What are you going to do?" he screamed. More thrashing about.

She held the skewer in a now gloved hand and

started to heat the end of it. "Wouldn't want you getting an infection, now would we?" The metal spike getting hotter, slowly turning an amber glow.

"No," he was pleading. "I didn't do anything. I have money. I can give you money."

"Sorry, bucko," she said. "Looking for other people's money today." She rounded the table so she was standing at his head. Looking down, upside down, at him. Their eyes met, briefly for a second, and then she plunged the heated metal spike down into his eye hole. The hissing of fluid on hot metal lasting a split second before she pushed it all the way in, ruining his eye in a flash of white light as she stirred it. The eyeball being eviscerated in a second, his screaming, attempts to flail as she held his head as still as she could.

Then a sudden stop.

"He's out," she said. Happened frequently, when people had major damage to something that wasn't going to kill them. The brain just shut down, unable to comprehend the things that were happening to it. Gel removed the spike from the meat's eye and held the skin open, so Raymond could zoom in and show the audience the damage. The hole in his face was full of pus, yellow bile mixing with red gloop.

Mike looked at the screen. The hole in the man's face. It *was* real. Fuck. His stomach stirred a little. *Fuck*. He'd just done that to this guy. He'd paid someone to fucking blind him.

Fuck.

His stomach turned a little as he studied the man's wrecked face. His handiwork.

But his cock turned too.

Gel waved the smelling salts under his nose with one hand and wiped roughly at his face with a rag in the other. Pushing the drools of juice from his face so the camera could pick up his terror. He heaved air in suddenly as consciousness awoke within him and he cried out. Pain ravaging his body, face, and hand. He wailed, realising he was blinded in one eye. He twisted and turned.

"And we're back," she said.

"We had two thousand for a hobbling."

"What the fuck's a hobbling?" She glanced to Raymond. He already had his phone in his hand, looking it up.

"According to this," he said. "It's crushing bones in the ankles or feet."

Gel shrugged. "Sounds good to me." She went to the kit and got the small sledgehammer. "Could have just said though." She went back to the meat, sledge in hand. He wasn't even paying attention. His brain firing left and right in fear. Pain. Incomprehension.

She raised the hammer. It was heavy. Hard to control. She'd used it plenty of times before though. Aimed.

She brought it down on the meat's foot. He was laying on his back, the foot pointing upwards, toes towards the ceiling. The weight alone was going to break something, but Gel had upper body strength behind it too. The lump of metal crushed the bones in the toes, breaking them up with ease, but carried on forward, into the foot itself. A long shard of the metatarsals slipping easily through the flesh and skin, protruding like a dagger.

The meat just made this noise like a pneumatic drill.

"Both?" she asked. Glancing at Raymond.

His glance went to the screen to check. Then he nodded at her.

She did the second. Blood flowing from the wounds, his feet destroyed by the impact.

Mike looked at the screen, a maniacal grin on his face. He watched the nice SS lady destroy the man's feet. The message had popped up on his screen, telling him what someone else had *purchased*. This was truly … disturbing. This was what he wanted, even without knowing what he wanted.

He typed in, "The penis. Take the penis. 1000."

Raymond shook his head. "That's not enough."

Gel dropped the hammer to the floor at the foot of the table, the blood gushing down from the meat's wrecked feet. Bones jutting out. Globs of fast clotted blood clumping, then dropping to the floor. She looked at its face. Gone again. "He's fucking passed out again," she hissed. She glanced over to Raymond. Saw the look of concentration on his face. "What's happening?"

He shook his head. "We're losing them." He gave her a quick look. "Bloke called Horse wants his hands off."

"How much?" she asked, sidling off camera.

"Two grand."

"No fucking way are we finishing *this* for *that*."

Raymond typed responses in frantically trying to get the amounts up, but no one seemed to budge. "The cock," he said. "Cut it off."

"For?" She didn't move towards the meat. Belligerent. No way was she putting on a show for next to no take home. Fuck that. She'd rather just leave him there like that to bleed out.

"One."

Gel looked from Raymond to the cock of the meat. "While he's out?"

"Guy didn't say. So yes. Whatever's easiest. Look. You might need to put on a fuck show at this rate."

Gel snorted, going to the kit and getting one of the craft knives. "I don't think he's going to be getting a hard-on anytime soon, and if you think I'm doing a solo show on a corpse for less than twenty grand you have another thing coming."

Raymond smiled. Her solo shows were certainly worth that, true.

She took the knife to the table and smiled at the camera. Never break character, not for the audience. She lifted his cock up. Even soft, a handful. Greggs sausage roll. That sort of thing. She eye fucked the audience for a moment. Teasing them. Teasing the cock from this blacked out chunk of meat. Her attention back to it.

Raymond agreed with Baller to take the cock. He watched the dude on the screen. New blood was hungry for it. That was good, so long as he didn't blow his load too soon.

"Well?" said Horse.

"More," he replied.

Horse dropped out of the Red Room.

"Fuck," he muttered. He scanned around the faces. Most of whom seemed more passive than usual. He glanced over to Gel.

She had the knife at the root of the meat's cock. Gently slipping it into the skin, showing how sharp the knife was. Before she pushed it through. Harder. Slipping into it like butter. A goo of clear liquid slipped out of it. Looked like pre-cum, then it spat out. Blood. Spitting like venom from a snake. The meat cried out, she looked, but he was still out. Screaming in his sleep.

Bless him.

She sawed through, until his cock was in her hand, but away from the rest of him. Holding it up to the camera. She didn't watch, hearing the piss spatter to the floor, mixing with the other fluids. The blood. She waved it to the camera, before holding it up, above her like she was going to fellate it. Fuck it with her face. She waved a finger to the camera. *Uh-uh*. You're not getting that. She mussed her fingers together, the sign for money. Pay to play. She glanced to Raymond.

He shook his head.

"Only thing on the table is two grand for a kill."

"Fuck," she whispered. She returned to the camera. "You wanna watch me fuck myself?" She ground for the camera. Looked into it, deep, like she was going to come for it. Wanted *it* to come for her. "You want to see me out of uniform?" Her hands twisted down the SS uniform, she moved like a stripper, talked like a whore. "You need to put something more on the table, boys and girls."

Raymond was still shaking his head.

She left the camera. To the kit. "Accept it. I'm done." She picked up the bone saw.

Raymond glanced to her. Then back to the camera. Eyes everywhere. Trying to see some punter that might put his hand in his pocket. They needed more money than this. They *needed* it. He looked at Horse. Seemed settled with his offer. Baller was touching himself. Over his trousers. Thankfully. But he was getting off on just watching. Couldn't boot him out the show though. Not after he'd paid for something.

That was it.

"Anyone not bought an item in tonight's show doesn't get to see the finale."

Two of the cameras went black as the clients fled the Red Room, upset that they weren't getting a free show. Raymond glanced to Gel. She was already striding to the meat. Saw up. She wasn't even going to tease. Not enjoy it. She was pissed off. Raymond started dropping people from the room. One after another. Those refusing to offer for anything, being dropped from the room, calling Raymond's bluff. Fuck them.

Gel went to the meat. His eyes were open and he was staring around the ceiling. Gone, mentally, she was sure. Half bled out and pushed to insanity by the pain. She grabbed his arm. Looked into his face. He didn't see her. "Sorry," she said. "Sorry you weren't worth more."

Then she dropped the saw onto the inside of his wrist and started to draw it back. The teeth pulling the skin at first, before tearing it. Not cutting. Ripping. She pushed down on it as she punched it forward. The teeth of the saw digging in deep with no effort, down through the flesh, the arteries, the veins, to the bone. Blood quelling on the wound, filling it, and rolling over the top. The last of his arterial pressure pushing it out.

She dragged it across the bone, the change in material making it harder, sweat beading on her forehead. "Damn it," she muttered. She looked at his cock, discarded to his belly. "Might have known he was going to be big boned." She dragged the saw, back and forth, the bones squealing, and crunching, before popping it through to the other side. It slipped through the rest of the flesh and out. The hand coming away, plopping to the floor amidst the blood and piss.

She looked at the camera and winked. That was all it was getting. Cheap skate motherfuckers. Then she rounded the table. Meat was gone again. Unconscious. It might even die before she got this one off. Didn't care now. Time to go.

Mike watched the hand come off. It was mesmerising. Seeing these people eviscerate another human being. Something like he'd never encountered before. Just … *God*. What the fuck? He wanted … more. "How much for a live show?" he asked.

Raymond looked at the question. "You've got to be kidding me," he muttered.

Gel looked up from the half-sawn second hand. "What?"

"Baller wants to come and watch."

Gel focussed back on the sawing. What if he did? Was that so … unreasonable? "How much?" she asked.

"That's what he's asking."

She slipped the saw through the rest of the meat's wrist and it dropped to the floor. Second arm didn't bleed as much as the first, understandably, but she'd not taken any care with the job. She was splattered with blood. Her uniform looking like she'd actually been in the SS, and the blood of the people was on her. She dropped the saw to the floor without ceremony, and walked off camera. Over to Raymond. "Show's over," she said, huffing air out. "That was hard." She looked down at the screen. The only person still connected was Baller. "He serious?"

"I think so." Baller was looking at the screen intensely, but Raymond could see the nervous energy in his eyes. "We need to make a call. Or we're going to lose him."

"How much do we need?"

"After tonight another fifteen should work." For now, he thought. *Until next time.*

"Tell him he can come. Join in. He has to join in. It'll be transmitted like the others. His face on camera. Twenty five."

Raymond shook his head. It was fucking madness. "He's new blood, he might be a fucking copper."

"We *need* the money." She jabbed her finger at the screen. At Baller. "Do it, before you lose him."

"Twenty five," Raymond typed. "But there are caveats."

Mike looked at the response. It was going to empty him out. Totally. But it had to be worth it. For sure. A fucking real show. Once in a lifetime. A notification pinged up on the bottom of the screen. Email from Bree. The fuck? He turned his attention back to the Red Room. "Caveats?" he asked.

The guy or woman or whoever the fuck he was talking to listed them out.

He had to be on camera. Had to be seen. It was insurance. Of course it was. He really shouldn't expect anything else. Fuck it. He had to say yes. Had to. If he didn't would he even be able to find his way back here. He needed this. "Done," he said. "How do we proceed?"

"I'll contact you," Raymond said.

"Fucking hell," Gel whispered. She glanced

around the room. "Better get on," she said.

"Yeah," Raymond replied. He opened a prompt and started typing. "I need to nail this guy while I have access to his I.P. I won't be long. He switched to the chat with Baller. "One second." Then back to the prompt. He was in. Into the guy's laptop. Opened his browser's history, his email. He looked at all the information in there. Back to the Chat. "Mike. I see your address, I have your contact details. We'll firm in a couple of days." Then he closed the laptop, killing the connection to the camera's, the feed. Killing the Red Room's existence.

"We got all the cash?"

"For what it's worth," he said. Pulling wires from the floor.

"We really gonna do this?" Gel asked.

"We don't have a whole lot of choice now. Do we?" He looked at her arse. A smear of blood going from the bottom of the uniform, onto her legs, clagging on the stockings. It was from where she'd touched herself. Turned him on. A little. But everything she did turned him on. A little.

Chapter 18

Bree sat alone at the dining table. She had a coffee sitting there. Her email to Mike sent, the one to Leslie saying that she didn't think she was coming back and that could she take her bag home and she'd arrange to collect it?

She looked at the time. It was early morning. Before two. She hadn't slept. Not since. She couldn't. It was weird. Every time she closed her eyes she could see his face. But also smell the breakfast. The pain, wrenching itself from her crotch.

Like he was still inside her.

Impossibly, still there.

And she couldn't shake it. A yawn escaped her, her body barely able to function. She sipped the coffee. The smell of coffee didn't help either. She blinked it away. Tried to focus on something else. She needed another job, she supposed. She had a few grand in the bank, but it wasn't going to last long. Not with the rent and everything else. A few months. Maybe a little longer. She should do the maths, but she really couldn't be bothered.

She thought about Mike. Just for a moment. A flicker of sadness at sending him a *Dear John* email.

Then she remembered the times he'd only wanted her when *he* wanted her. The sex. Rough sex at times. Rougher than she would have liked it. Then his distant cold after he'd finished.

Finished with her.

Like he was a different person before they had sex to after. A bully, though. For sure. Why she hadn't fucked him off before was almost a mystery.

She stirred her coffee absently. Her mind's eye then to *him* again. She probably wasn't even going to get a reference, was she?

Chapter 19

"So," said Gel, "how are we going to do it?"

"I have idea's ploughing around the grey stuff." Raymond indicated from the traffic lights, pulling around perfectly. One mile an hour below the speed limit. An example of perfect driving.

They'd been pulled over once, on the way back from a shoot. Fucking spot check bullshit. They were looking to nab someone for drink driving. Breathalysed him and everything. By that time they were over a hundred miles from the shoot, so he never worried that they were going to put two and two together later, and realise that them driving about was going to be the same them that had butchered an old man in a warehouse.

But the whole time he watched Gel. She looked like she was going to shit. She kept looking to the boot. The boxes in there. Full of bloody clothes. She was high as a fucking kite the whole time. It was a miracle that the fuzz didn't catch on.

"We'll need a spot near where he is. I can't risk dragging him over the country."

"Is that wise? If he gets picked up for it, then he'll just drop us in it for any deal they put on the table."

"Yeah, but it's that, or we cut him loose straight after and hope he's not stupid enough to get himself caught, or we ferry him home, drive three quarters of the way around the country in one night. With a boot full of evidence. The best thing we do, is we do what we do, the way we do it. Play it like he's not there. We've never been caught yet, have we?"

Gel stared out the window as they pulled onto the motorway. Clear of the smaller streets, she pulled a baggie of whizz and drew a crude line of it on a takeout menu from the glove box. The vacuum sound as she snorted it. Then back up. Looking out the window like nothing had happened. "Okay. What about the meat? You got a tag on this guy yet, so I can start that? And what do you want? What's *he* gonna want?"

"I already have a bead on him. Got it at the shoot. Cracked his accounts. Don't worry about the meat. He's getting what he's given. And I have it in hand."

Gel watched some arseface slam by doing over a hundred in a fucking pox sized car. "You better be right about this."

Raymond glanced over to her. Yeah. He had better be. All he had to do, was do what he did. Do it for her. Pay off the bastards. Maybe then, they could run. Another country. Somewhere that he could get her clean.

He looked in the rear view.

There was a police car in the distance. Flashing lights.

Fuck.

He slowed, pulling over to the left. Waiting to see how it was going to play out. The car smashed past them. Following the other, probably. He could feel his heart hammering inside his chest. He looked at her. Eyes wide. The speed increasing her flow of thought.

"Can we stop for a burger?" she asked.

Raymond shook his head, blinking the question away. "No," he said, incredulously. "No, of course we can't."

She huffed. "Fine." Arms crossed across her chest. Eyes wide.

She wasn't going to sleep through this one, but at least if she was going to be bratty she was probably going to do it quietly. Raymond looked at the speedo and made sure to keep it respectable. He had an idea. It was still forming, but it was going to work.

Chapter 20

Mike stared at the screen. The room long dead. He hadn't moved. He hadn't done anything. Just sat there. Thinking. What had he done?

He felt like he'd just paid over the odds for an ebay auction and now was wishing he hadn't, even though he really did want the item. He'd just bought a kill. A murder. Something he was going to have to do. On camera. For the whole world to see.

But like ebay, he didn't think he could change his mind. Not now. They had his name. Knew where he lived. All in seconds. Just like the dealers before. If he tried to back out, then they'd come for him. Of course they would.

Maybe that was what the guy with the big dick had done. Maybe he'd fucked them around and they just grabbed him. Took him to whatever place *that* was and fucking murdered him.

He pushed himself away from the screen. Looked at the wall. Maybe that place was a studio that they grabbed people off the street and took them to, some underground lair, and they disappeared, permanently. He drew air in. He'd empty his bank account for this. He snorted. A look to the work laptop. One for a job he didn't have anymore. They were sending IT over to pick it up in the morning.

Shit. He would probably need a job now. But it was worth it. Right? Of course it was. He stood.

Realised for the first time he still had a hard-on. Fucking hell. He took it, in his hand, through his sweats. Stroked himself absently while he walked in a circle in the living room. Going to kill someone. Going to do it on camera. While people watched.

He could feel himself come close to orgasm. So quick. Because fuck knows how long he'd been hard. He stopped. His cock crying out to be finished, but he went to the computer. Opened his email. There was something from Bree. Fuck that. He could read that tomorrow. Eyes down to the time. Fucking three in the morning. It wasn't like he could just booty call her now. She wasn't like that. Didn't want to fuck all the time. He stroked himself again. Maintained his erection. Opened some porn and let it play.

Staring at it.

Through it.

He was thinking about the show. The one he'd just watched. The woman in the uniform. She was fucking hot. Sexy. Stockings, dirty ones. Holes in them. A Nazi fucking uniform. Hat and everything. He listened to the sound of the porn, people fucking on the screen. Closed his eyes and thought about her. Over him. He was tied to the table. Like that loser was. But he was tied to the table and they were gonna fuck. She opened her uniform, drawing open the buttons slowly. Straddled across him. His cock resting against her wet panties. He'd seen her panties. He imagined the smell of them, as she undid the last button and opened the jacket. Her body, beneath. Naked.

Mike opened his eyes. His cock sticky, he'd come in his sweats.

"Shit," he muttered. Lost, he didn't even feel it.

He closed the porn, and got up. Cold and hard in

his clothes. Cum. Running down him. He went to the bathroom and pulled his clothes off. His cock still hard. Hadn't come properly. Just half-heartedly. He turned the shower on. Got under the water, and closed his eyes, stroking himself again.

Chapter 21

Gel lay in bed, still. Raymond at the laptop. He was sitting in the chair in the corner of the bedroom, one eye on her, one on the screen. After they'd gotten home she'd just crashed. Hard. He'd gone to grab a beer, and when he came back she was on the sofa. Out like a light. He'd picked her up and come in here. Put her into the bed. She'd barely stirred. He stripped her naked, and pulled the covers over her. A longing glance at her body. That was hours ago.

He was looking through the new client's emails. Reading them. Making notes of what he needed to. He lived down on the coast. Slimy little town. He'd walked about the high street on Google Maps. The place didn't look like it had any money. But that was okay. Raymond had already used the information on Mike's computer to open his bank account and see how much money he *did* have.

Which wasn't much more than he said he'd pay.

Fine. If he wanted to empty his life savings out for a few hours of jollies that was up to him. But it also meant that the two of them couldn't lean on him for more. Extras. Fucking Gel. Or him. Probably Gel, looking at the type of porn the guy looked at, although he did seem to like looking at *other things* occasionally.

He shook the thought from his head. He hated thinking about pimping her out. He'd rather do it himself. But with that bank balance, it was off the table anyway.

Gel turned. A grunt became a moan. "Honey," she said.

"I'm here."

"Coffee."

He smiled. Put the laptop to the side and left to the kitchen. Put the kettle on while he stared at the wall. He needed a studio for the shoot. Somewhere local to the client. There was miles of fucking fields down that side of the country. Shouldn't be hard. The washing machine rolled over, spinning again. He looked down to it. Thrashing around with her uniform in. He was exhausted. Hadn't even gotten into bed yet. The kettle clicked off and he poured the drink. Took it into the bedroom.

She hadn't moved. Hopefully she hadn't gone to sleep again.

He went to her side of the bed and put the mug down. She opened her eyes. Those and the top of her head, the only thing visible under the sheets. A cheeky grin. "You been up long?"

Raymond smiled down at her. "Just a while."

She snaked her hand out and reached up to his junk. Squirming it over his jeans. "Why don't you jump back in here?"

His smile didn't waver. "I just need to get some more work done."

She made a pouty face.

Raymond shook his head. "We need to get this shit cleared up once and for all, and with what little we did make last night, if we can get this Mike guy secured, we can probably make a deal to pay Luca off."

She sighed. A little seriousness behind the eyes.

Like she really did understand that this was largely her doing. "What about stripping his bank account? I take it you've already checked to make sure he's good for it."

Raymond nodded. "Yeah, and he is, but we've been through this before. We don't do that. The paper trail on cyber crime is easier to follow than the paper trail of a massacre at the Andrex warehouse. I don't want to change things. Things work the way they are."

She rubbed his junk again. "Daddy doesn't like change."

He laughed. His cock was happy to move back to the bed, but his big head wasn't there. It was tied up in the best way to move forward. This was all new ground. Something he'd never seen anyone on the circuit attempt before.

Raymond returned to the chair and sat, pushing the laptop onto his lap, and opening a new window. He started looking over the maps of the areas surrounding the town this Mike guy lived in. He didn't want to travel too far. Not with either Mike or the meat.

Chapter 22

Two days later

Mike looked himself down in the mirror. So preoccupied with his look that the sound of porn coming too loudly from the TV was of no concern. His neighbours could probably hear it. Hell, they could probably hear it in the street. The guy he'd been talking to—he should clarify, he had no idea if it was a guy or not. They had never *spoken*. All communication had been done through chats and emails. It was an assumption. One based on little. He assumed that there were only two of them, which may or may not be accurate. The girl in the uniform. The one that did all the work, she didn't look big enough to be containing guys and tackling them to the ground. Bundling them into the back of vans. So he assumed a *he*. Called himself Red.

Very inventive.

He was told to wear something appropriate. No idea what that meant, so he'd been out earlier that day and picked around in some charity shops. Gotten some disposable black clothing. Something he didn't mind losing.

He was now looking at himself in the mirror. He looked like a stone cold killer. Fucking brutal. Fucking *cool*.

Checking his phone he saw that it was nearly

time. They already had his address. Fuck it. They already had the money. Red told him if he didn't transfer the cash to bitcoin and then dump it over to him hours before, then a) they wouldn't pick him up, and b) they would take the money anyway. And he believed that they could. They seemed to know everything about him, and yet he'd told them nothing. Fucking hackers. All of them.

Equally, he didn't feel like he had any reason to distrust them.

They wanted the money, and if they could take it anyway, why hadn't they, if they were going to rip him off? So everything was on track, right? He'd paid the money, and was ready.

He stalked to the window and looked out. Red told him that they would pick him up in a red Mondeo. They'd pull up outside at five. He had to be out the door in less than two minutes or they were leaving.

He looked from the road to his phone again.

Okay.

He took a breath, a single glance down himself. He was as ready as he could be. Nervous, though. He was going to do it. Actually fucking do it.

Murder someone.

He rolled his phone in his hand, the sweat on his palm transferring to the screen and beading. *Piece of cake*. The thrill of it. That was what he wanted. And so what if people all over the world watched? They were going to be in as much trouble as him. He wanted the final kill. Didn't want her to do it. But then, he'd paid, so he should get what he wanted, right? He'd need to make that clear. Without pissing Red off, of course. He didn't want to get murdered himself. Not for being pushy. There was a horn from outside, getting his attention back to the road.

He looked down the street, both ways. No Mondeos. Wiped his phone down his trousers, and pushed it in his pocket. "Come on," he whispered.

Wanted to get started.

Excited. He could feel pee pushing against his bladder. "Not now," he hissed. No way was he missing this because he was having a pee.

A Mondeo pulled up. Outside his flat. On the double yellows.

A red one.

Mike looked at the vehicle, trying to see through the net curtains to the passenger. The car was idling on the wrong side of the road, so he couldn't see the driver. Her. He was sure he could see her hair. Wow. She was in the car too. Waiting for him. "Fuck," he whispered to himself, nearly falling over the sofa as he turned. Mike picked up the remote to the TV on the way past and flicked it off. Hurried across the room, to the front door. Out into the hallway. He slammed his front door. The chick from upstairs was standing at their front door. Looked pissed. Like they were about to complain about the noise.

"Fucking hell, Mike," she said.

Mike stared through her. Lost at what she was talking about. "Sorry," he said, absently. Then turned to the front of the building, out.

He didn't have time to talk to people. He couldn't miss his lift.

He hurried to the side of the car and bent down to the window. She was so fucking hot in real life. The camera did her no justice, and he would have paid for time with her, even with her looking like she did on camera. But like this?

"Well?"

He looked across her to the driver. Fuck. Shouldn't just stand there and stare. "Hi," he said. "I'm Mike."

The driver just stared at him. Mouth open in some sort of look of horror.

"Get *in*," the woman hissed.

"Oh, right." Mike got in the back, behind the woman, and slid across to the middle. The driver stopped the hazard warning lights on the car, and indicated out.

"Put your belt on," he ordered. He looked in the mirror, his eyes meeting Mike's.

"Right," Mike said. Bewildered at the need for road traffic safety, when they were on their way to eviscerate someone. But he slid back behind the passenger seat and pulled his seat belt on, regardless.

Then the driver pulled out.

Into the traffic. Calm and collected. Like he was taking his kid to football practice or some shit. Mike watched the world pass, as they drove along towards the centre. The high street.

"So," he said, a sudden need to break the silence. "Good drive down?"

The driver—who Mike keenly assumed was Red—looked at him in the mirror again. "Fine," he replied. "twenty-five was busy."

"Oh," Mike said. "You've come that far."

"We come from all over," the woman said, joining in.

"Mike," Mike said, introducing himself, again. His hand went out, over the seat, but she just looked at it. He withdrew it, before she answered.

"Gel," she said. She open hand, back-hand slapped the driver's arm. "This big lug is Red. Raymond."

"Raymond," Mike acknowledged, clearing his throat. "So …" the words died in his throat. He looked back out the window. They were heading out of town. To be expected. "Are we going to your place?"

Raymond looked in the mirror without word again. The look on his face told Mike everything he needed to know, though. Raymond thought Mike was an imbecile. Fine. He could live with that. As long as he got what he wanted.

Gel turned in the seat and looked at him. She was chewing gum. Made her look like a sex symbol. Not that she needed the gum for that. Mike could easily picture her as his girl. When he blinked, she was naked. They were fucking. Christ. He looked from her, out through the windscreen, and then back to her. Must be an adrenaline overdose.

No turning back now. He was here. Kill, or he assumed, be killed. Money paid. He was on the ride. She was speaking. Shit. Mike focussed on her.

"Silly," she said. "We're doing this local for you. So you don't need to travel. We don't ever do anything at ours." She giggled. It was cute. "Well, nothing illegal." Giggled again.

Mike didn't get the joke.

"We're going to the set." Raymond finally spoke. "Once we're there you'll get to see us set up. All part of the experience. Then we'll go and get the meat. You'll have to wait at the set and guard it."

Guard it. Fucking hell. Mike was really important in this. He felt his chest swell. Gel was watching him, still. He felt something else swell, too. He cursed himself. Nodding like he was paying attention. Best not look sideways at her. What if these two were fucking? He didn't want to end up in a hole in the ground for making a pass at a ... they were serial killers, he supposed ... serial killer's lay. He looked at Raymond. He was older than Gel. Didn't mean anything. Not these days. They could still be doing it.

His eyes crossed to Gel, as she turned and righted herself in the seat.

Actually, in retrospect. *She* was a serial killer. Fuck. What did he know? Maybe Raymond was in front of the camera sometimes. Gestapo uniform, maybe. "The meat?" he said. "Is that the ..." He hoped someone would finish the sentence for him.

"Yes," Raymond said. He sounded impatient.

"Do you know what I'm getting?" Mike ventured. He did hope that he wasn't pissing these two off. Maybe stop asking questions.

"We always have an idea about the meat," he continued. "Gel usually arranges a date over some hookup app, and we grab them in a suitable location. Doesn't really matter what we get as long as it meets the niche requirements of the clients, but we rarely know what that's going to be, so it's a game of odds."

Mike nodded along like he understood. It sort of made sense. Sort of. He looked back out the window, deciding that quietness was on the menu. They'd passed the edge of town and were in between the fields. Near the estate.

The car turned off the main road, and into a side street. Between two fields.

Mike watched. A farmhouse in the distance. Getting closer. The only thing out there. The house. Something that looked like a barn to the side of it. Graffiti up the outside of it. Even from there he could see the windows were all blown out. Place looked abandoned.

That was probably the point though.

Raymond took the car up the side between the house and the barn and stopped the engine. He turned around to Mike, arm over the seat. Like he was his dad and he was going to tell him about the birds and the bees. "Look," he said. "The game plan is simple. We set up. Go get the meat. Do the show. You are going to get what you want, but let me make it clear. You turn on us in any way and you'll be tomorrow's matinee. And that goes from now, forever. I will never not be watching you. A single step out of line. Get it?"

Mike nodded.

Raymond turned back to face forward, but stopped himself. Like he'd remembered something. "Also, I know what Gel does for you boys. That's part of the show. You look at her funny, and I will personally make sure it's the last thing you do."

She reached over and touched Raymond's arm. A small smile. Loving. Caring.

So they *were* fucking. Good to know.

Then Raymond got out of the car. He went straight to the building, disappearing in. Gel and Mike still there. Gel watched him enter the building, before pushing her door open. She opened the glove box. Started fiddling with some powder in a baggie and a takeout menu.

Mike watched, then decided not to watch. Then tried to look like he wasn't watching, while he was.

She offered the menu forward to him.

Mike shook his head. No idea what the powder was. Best not start a drug habit today. No. He needed to be on his best game. Not only remember everything perfectly, cast into memory, but also so he didn't do something stupid. He opened the door and stuck his feet out. Didn't want to end up in the bushes over there with no penis.

He pushed himself up, as Raymond came from the house, and went to the barn. Raymond paying neither of them any mind. He was busy. Making sure they were alone, Mike assumed. Alone and safe.

He came from the barn building a few moments later and waved over to the two of them. Gel got out the car and Mike followed suit. He was intrigued by it. It was all very organised. He wondered how many times they'd done it before, but decided not to ask.

The bushes over there still very much at the front of his mind.

Gel opened the boot and started collecting stuff into her arms. "Little help," she said. "But be careful. This shit's expensive."

Mike went to the boot, standing behind her, waiting his turn to help with *this shit*. Queuing because he was British. Looking at her arse because he was horny.

Raymond cleared his throat and Mike's attention went from the very nice arse to the very staring at him, Raymond. Mike looked at the floor and hoped he wasn't going to die that night. "So," he said, trying to take Raymond's attention anywhere else. "How'd the two of you get into all this?"

Raymond frowned as Gel handed him a couple of bags. "Desperation," he said.

Mike noticed Raymond's eyes following Gel as he said that. Like subconsciously it was her fault he had to do this and he somewhat resented it. Then he noticed that he was staring at her disappearing into the building and Raymond was watching him. Again. Mike quickly turned to the boot and started pulling things out.

Carefully.

Chapter 23

They both seemed to know what they were doing, and Mike found himself more an adornment to the corner of the room than anything else. Watching them set up the studio. Raymond had clearly done this a thousand times. He even managed to plug in USB things the first time. There was a generator, one that had come from the boot of the car. It was organised. Military, even, with little more than a second wasted as they got everything in its place.

Then Raymond stood. "Okay," he said. "I'm leaving you in charge of the set. The equipment. All of it. It's worth thousands, so don't touch anything. When we get back, you'd better still be here, and this had better still be here. We've never lost equipment, and it would be a shame if we were to lose some the only night we have a third."

There was no threat in the words, but Mike knew that Raymond was trying to intimidate him.

It was working.

But he also had no intention of fucking anything up. They knew fucking everything about him, and they already had all his money, and he was here for one reason alone. The *meat*. He wanted it. He wanted to be there. Do it. So he nodded along, and when Raymond had finished, he just said, "Gotcha."

A smile. You can trust me, it said.

Raymond's face said that he didn't.

Raymond looked at Mike standing in the doorway of the building waving them goodbye, as he reversed the Mondeo out of the yard. What a cunt. "Look at him," he muttered.

Gel snorted. "Yeah. Like a little puppy."

"You really think he's got what it takes to do this?"

Gel shrugged. She didn't really care. They had the money, and she had seen the relief rising in Raymond's shoulders now they did. They just needed to get this done, and get Mike back home, without any entanglement with anyone else, and they were home free. And you know what? If they pulled this together tonight, and everything went to plan, then she was going to make a real effort to clean up. "If he hasn't I can still do it."

Raymond indicated the car out, and onto the main road. "You know there is a good chance that as soon as this goes public there are going to be a whole bunch of people asking to do the same. Thinking this is some pay to ride gig."

"The thought had crossed my mind." She watched the street lights flickering on as they passed. "But once we clear Luca we can either make bank or fuck off."

"I was thinking of fucking off."

"Lot of money to leave behind."

"Lot of risk too." Raymond smiled to himself. He was ready for the stress and pressure of the job to rise from him. It was going to need a big payday to pull him back in after tonight.

Gel watched the town coming as they headed back in. "This isn't going to be the easiest pick up in the world, either."

"You never know your luck."

Mike stood there in the dim light of the backup lighting. The main lights were off while they were out. He was standing over the table that they'd set up for the meat. A kit of tools on the smaller table just off camera next to it. The fleeting thought that they were just going to leave him there and call the police, claiming him to be some psycho serial killer, was now gone once he'd thought out the business end of it. He stepped away from it all and looked at the equipment. Keyboards and laptops. Routers. Internet things he didn't understand. But he didn't go near it. Wasn't about to risk that.

He pulled his phone and looked at the time as he strolled to the next room. Designated as the changing room, Mike had been told not to go in there. Just a peek. Wouldn't harm. He looked at the uniform that Gel was going to wear. The same as the one she wore last time. When she killed that guy. Cut his dick off. Still staring at it, Mike swallowed back his saliva. Excitement in him. Raring to go. He glanced at the other things there. There was a schoolgirl uniform too. Must be for the meat.

Did that mean he was getting a girl?

Good. He wanted a girl. Didn't want to have to handle some guy's prick just because some faceless guy on the internet wanted him too. Although, he'd paid. He should get to say what he does and what he doesn't do. That only seemed fair.

He turned out of the changing room.

Better not get caught in there.

Raymond slipped from the car. Before leaning against it. He looked around. Casual, like. Pretending that it was the most normal thing in the world, him being there, leaning against a car.

Lucky the Mondeo wasn't a complete piece of shit, because this area was a damn sight nicer than the shit side of town they'd picked up Mike in. He leant there for a moment. Even just this, early evening, the road was quiet. There was money there.

Nice places. Probably had security too. He left the car, pushing himself from the door, and knocked on the window as he did. Gel got out on the signal and rounded the car to him. The two of them standing on the path. Chatting.

Saying goodnight to each other.

Doing what people do when they say goodnight to each other. After work. Whatever. What the fuck did they know, anyway? Gel slipped from him, her hand slipping out of his, and she went to the side of the building and around.

Raymond waited a moment, then he followed.

The two of them going around the back of the block of flats. Nice communal garden around there. Benches and shit. Grim in the darkness. But fine. The meat lived on the ground floor. Gel was already at the open window when Raymond came around and he went to her. Nice area. No worries about leaving windows open for a little fresh air. Even if the room beyond was empty. It was a stupid risk, he wasn't going to deny that, but this area looked as nice as the area they lived in, and he would never leave open unattended windows. He boosted himself up. Slipped in with the agility of a man younger than himself. Helped Gel up and in with him. Into the bedroom. Woman's bedroom. Pink and girly.

Which surprised Raymond. He couldn't stop himself from looking at the sheets and soft toys and shit. He didn't know what he was expecting, but certainly not this. He shook the thought and went to the door, listening. There were lights underneath. Good. Waiting. He pushed his hand in his jacket pocket and pulled the syringe pouch. Got one out. Gel waiting patiently.

The nod went down. They were ready.

Door open. Into the flat.

Raymond heard the car approach. He pushed his phone back into his pocket, flicking the app closed from the bottom of the screen. He knew he was supposed to be keeping a lookout, but he'd bored pretty quickly.

He was playing a game of cards. His attention on that.

When the car idled to a stop, he shook himself out. Beads of sweat on his brow even though it wasn't a warm night. Clammy. He looked through the window. Raymond and Gel manhandling someone out the boot. Body wasn't moving. He was still hoping the uniform was for a *her*. He didn't want it to be weird if it was a him.

They brought the body to the building and through into the changing room. Not even acknowledging him. He stood. Trying not to look. Trying not to try to look. It should be a surprise. He wanted it to be a good surprise. He was going to see her before the camera's were on, right? He didn't want to have *present face* on camera. Oh. Yes. Big hairy bloke. Yay. Just what I wanted.

It didn't matter, he told himself. He would deal with a bloke. Just preferred a woman. You never knew—if he did a good job they might ask him back. He paced back and forth, before stopping at the changing room. "You need a hand?" he asked, hopefully.

"No," Raymond responded dryly.

Mike sighed. Paced again

Chapter 24

Mike was behind the laptops and everything else. They were refusing to let him see the meat until the show was ready. He was getting anxious. Angry, even. If this was some fucking joke, he was not going to be impressed. Pull back the curtain as it were, to find a fucking goat under there or something. He watched across the room, the meat secured to the table. Under a sheet. Raymond sitting at the laptops, dicking with shit.

Gel coming out from the changing room in the SS uniform.

Fucking. Hell. Mike stared at her. Didn't care if Raymond was looking at him. He wanted her. He really fucking wanted her. Any fucking red-blooded mammal was going to want her, and Raymond had to understand that.

"Hot, right?"

Mike looked at Raymond staring at him. "Uh huh," he replied, barely able to contain his excitement. Fucking ... her there, like that, and the meat, ready under the sheet. "Yeah," he continued.

"You excited?"

"A little."

Raymond laughed. "This bit is always exciting. Did we tranq the meat too hard and is it dead? Will someone walk by the set and hear the meat's blood curdling screams? Will the armed police turn up and gun us all down?" He looked at Mike's face as it gurned into horror. "It's okay. We're good at what we do. None of those things have happened." He turned back to the laptop. Added, "*Yet.*" Smiling as Mike seemed to tighten.

"She should be ready soon," Gel said.

Raymond tapped a few keys.

The Red Room was open.

Now Streaming

"What does it look like?" Gel came behind the laptops to the two of them.

"Busy," Raymond replied. "I told everyone we had a surprise."

She leant in closer. Mike unsure what either of them were looking at, but his attention more on the sheet than the laptops. "I think she's waking up," he said.

She's. Raymond shot him a look, wondering why that was his assumption if he hadn't peeked. But it was probably just what he was fantasising about, more than what he *knew* he was getting. Then he looked over to the meat. Her head was moving. He was right. "Showtime," he said.

Gel righted herself and took Mike by the hand, leading him to the stage. In front of the meat. Raymond rattling the keys. Telling the clients that they had a paid client with them. Engaging in the entertainment. Someone to help Gel along. It seemed to garner some interest.

Good.

The two of them stood there for a moment. Gel had let his hand go before they were on camera. Then she leant in and whispered to him. "You ready?"

Mike nodded. He was shitting it. It was completely understandable, he was telling himself. He was about to commit murder on camera for shits and giggles—having paid for it, which in the eyes of the law was probably worse somehow—and he had an erection that had just now popped up and hurt. "Yeah," he muttered, reinforcing his readiness, even if it was just to himself.

Then Gel stepped up to the sheet, leaving Mike there. Just behind. Watching. She looked at the camera. "Y'all ready for this one?" She said, oozing sex into the words. "This one's a doozy." Then she pulled the sheet back.

Mike sucked air in through his teeth. He looked at Bree in the tight schoolgirl outfit, pulling against the binds that held her down, gagged. Her torso writhing and aching under the uniform. She looked wildly around the room like a trapped animal, ignoring him completely. *Fuck*. His mind went completely blank for a split second. There were no thoughts … none … apart from how ridiculously hot she was.

Then all the thoughts—all of them—smashed him in the head like a freight train running a light.

Fuck. They'd grabbed Bree as the meat. With some unbelievably small odds, they'd pulled the chick that was trying to leave him, as the meat, for this online snuff film. Well. What are the chances?

He looked at Gel. She was staring at him, like she was waiting for him to do something. Was he supposed to start? Did he talk to the camera? He pleaded with his eyes for her to just *tell him what to do*.

"Well?" she said.

His eyes flickered down to Bree again. Yes, he thought. Well?

Then Bree's eyes dropped to him.

He looked in them as the panic that had been swelling nearly as hard as the swelling in his trousers seemed to lift, like she realised that this was all some prank, and a pathetic attempt to what, woo her over and get her back? Christ. He was prick, sure, but even he wouldn't have tried the *kidnap and rescue* bluff to win back some girl. He wasn't that desperate.

Then Gel pulled her gag out her mouth.

The room was unceremoniously silent.

Raymond watched the screens. His brag of there being something special tonight, and that he'd coded for a larger room had meant that a) he had a lot of clients waiting at the start, and b) there seemed to be a hum of excitement among them. There were both men and women, a good cross section of ages and everything from bankers to wankers. "Hero," he said. "Camera." The guy leant forward, and Raymond moved to the next. They seemed excited. The reveal of the girl in the uniform, it got the guy's blood rushing. Some of the girl's too.

He glanced over to Mike. He was hanging back, and none of them were speaking. His eyes dropped over to Gel. She was glaring at Mike waiting for him to say something. "Come on guys," he muttered.

Please don't say this was going to be an absolute fuck up.

Gel looked from Mike to Bree and back again. Well? *Well*? She cleared her throat. Looked at the camera. "You guy's see what I see?" she said. She put her best sex worker voice on for it. She was a little surprised that Bree hadn't spoken yet. She'd turned from bright red with the gag into pale as a leper with the gag out. Now she'd seen her ex. Her attention back to Mike, "Well?" she said.

"Yeah. I … uh … I know her."

He sounded like he didn't want to say it. Like she was an accident. Like of all the people in all the world, she had to walk into his Red Room. "I know," she hissed. "She dumped you, right?" But she looked at the camera. Winked.

Mike was looking at her. Wide eyed and somewhat bemused. "No. Well, yes. I mean she did dump me, but I … I …"

Gel looked knowingly into the camera. "His girlfriend dumped him and now she's tied to the table, waiting to see what he's going to do." She held her hand over her mouth, open, faux shock and awe. "What do you want to see happen?" She looked down Bree. Taut in the uniform. She had a hot fucking body, and Gel wasn't surprised that she'd dumped this loser. She was however surprised that she'd gotten with him in the first place.

And that was about when Bree seemed to fall in that this wasn't some redundant line in bullshit.

Mike stared down at her. She was beautiful. Of course she was beautiful. She was Bree. *His* Bree. "I … I don't …" he looked in her eyes as they sparked anger and hate. A mix of fear. Anguish. Rolling emotion. After what she said. That email. This was his perfect chance to get revenge. On camera.

For the world to see.

Shit. Surely having him killing her on camera was going to get him caught? But how would it? He was standing there, staring into the nothing. "Christ," he muttered. Realised he was shaking. He didn't know what to do. Just kill her. That was the best thing to do. *Just kill her*.

He looked around the room quickly. Over to the kit. All the tools of the trade. The murder implements.

Yes. That was it. Get it done. Over with. He turned and slipped off camera. A quick look to Raymond who was splitting his time between him and Gel, and the screen. He didn't look best pleased.

Mike picked up the knife. It was the easiest and most murdery thing he saw. Turned back to Bree on the table. Strode back.

"What the Hell do you think you're doing?" Gel barked. She glanced to the camera. A spark of anger. She got between him and Bree. Put her body in the way.

Stopped him dead in his tracks. He didn't want to hurt her. He wanted to fuck *her*. Fuck. He was so confused. He could feel the hard plastic of the knife handle in his palm. It was slipping around. Wet. Slick with his sweat. A shiver cut down him. "I'm going to kill her, like we agreed," he stuttered, the words barely getting out.

Gel stepped towards him. She looked pissed. "What the fuck? We need to do what the client's tell us," she hissed, trying to keep her voice down. "You can't go all Rambo on her."

"But I paid," he said. The room was spinning a little. He was spiralling. "I paid to kill her."

"You paid to be in front of the camera," she snapped. "Not to have a fucking free pass." She was eyeing the blade in his hand, wary that he could go fucking postal at any second.

"But I paid," he said again.

"You do what you're told," she barked. She was getting a little closer. Had a lot of her attention on the knife.

Raymond looked at the screen. Then over to Gel. That cunt, Mike. He was fucking everything up.

Getting his ex had been his idea. He saw the email—the one that came in while he still had access to Mike's computer when they were talking. It seemed like a fucking sure fire way of getting him to keep fucking quiet after the act. Hey, who wants to admit to butchering a lay that's told them where to stick it?

Perhaps it hadn't been such a hot idea to rummage about in his emails and find her address from some parcel delivery, and use her. Should have gone and gotten some whore off the street instead.

He looked at the screen. A couple of them had disconnected.

Back to the two of them. All he wanted to do was get Mike by the throat and squeeze. "We're losing the clients," he said.

"I don't care if you paid. It doesn't work like that," Gel hissed. She wasn't close enough to take the knife from him. But was close enough that if he lunged forward she wasn't going to be able to stop him. "Give me the knife."

He looked at it in his hand, then over her shoulder to Bree.

Gel shot a desperate look to Raymond, but his attention was going back and forth between them and the screen. He looked like he could murder someone.

"I paid you twenty five thousand for this privilege," Mike snapped.

"Fuck you," she replied. Shit. That came out wrong. The knife was twisting in his hand.

Raymond was up. Mike couldn't see him. He was crossing the floor behind him. Onto the set. Onto camera. Most unusual for Raymond.

But Gel appreciated it.

She glanced at the camera. There was fear there.

She didn't know what to do. This was a bomb. They had Mike's money. This was going to be the end of the show, clearly. Then Raymond was behind Mike, one hand on his wrist holding the knife, and the other under his chin, around his throat, like if this was an action film, he was going to snap his neck.

Gel actually had no idea what the plan was, but that Raymond was there, certainly put her mind at ease.

"I'll do it," the meat said.

Raymond squeezed Mike's wrist and twisted his arm. Banged his hand against the table, and the knife dropped.

"What?" Gel replied. She looked at the meat. The meat was speaking. Then she looked at Raymond.

"Get the fuck off me," Mike snapped.

"Swap me," Bree shouted over the ruckus. "I have the same amount of money. Fucking untie me and *I'll* do what the client's say."

Bree looked from the meat to Mike to Raymond. The room moving in slow motion. What the fuck was going on?

Raymond turned Mike and still from behind him, he pushed him over, bending him forward, quick and hard, slamming his forehead on the corner of the table. Mike dropped like a sack of rocks and sprawled unconscious on the floor. Raymond, breathing hard. He stepped over the prone body. "You all right?" he asked, pulling Gel into a hug. "Did he hurt you?"

"No," she said, squirming gently to be released, his arms strong on her, but she was aware they were on camera, she knew that some of the illusion was her sexuality.

"You can have it," Bree said. "Swap me with

him, and you can have it." She looked down herself, puffing air, cheeks out like a hamster. "Come on. I'll fucking enjoy it too."

Raymond released Gel and stepped back off camera. He went straight to the screens. Evaluate the damage. There were no other dropouts. Apparently the pushing and shoving hadn't damaged the entertainment any.

A message on the screen.

Lady said, "One thousand to see the meat get what she wants."

Raymond smiled.

A deep burning sensation in his head. A pulse thumping against his temple. Thoughts coagulating, stiff, thick. Mike opened his eyes. He was cold. *Real* cold. He was laying on the floor. Looking at the ceiling. Shit. What had happened? He must have fallen. Knocked his head on something. Why was he so cold? He tried to raise his head, but the blood in there was too heavy and the pain too bold. Instead he rolled his head to the side and looked across the room. He was too high to be on the floor. They must have picked him up and helped him onto something. He could see Raymond over there. Sitting behind the screens. And Gel. She was leant against the wall behind him. Talking to Bree. *Bree*.

Wow. She looked hot in that schoolgirl uniform. So tight. In all the right places.

He blinked.

Wait.

Gel had seen that he'd moved and was pointing at him. He realised that he couldn't hear anything. There was an incessant buzzing in his ears. Must have been from where he hit his head on the table. But he forced his head up. Looked down himself. He was naked apart from his pants. The same pants he was wearing under his black trousers. He couldn't move. He yanked at his arms, tried to move them. Pain spiked down from his wrists where he pulled against the binds holding him down.

"No," he said. The word came out muffled. He had something in his mouth. No. God. What's going on?

Gel came over. Bree still behind the cameras.

Mike saw the lights on the cameras. They were all still on. He was being shot. He was … oh. Oh *God*. No. Jesus fucking no. "Please," he tried to say. He was on the table. He was the meat now. They'd released Bree. In exchange for him.

Gel ripped the gag from him.

Made his jaw hurt. "I have more money," he blurted. "Swap me back."

"No," said Bree, "you don't."

"Don't listen to her," Mike continued. His words coming out with barely a space between them … *don'tlistentoher*.

"No," Raymond cut in. "You really don't. We know how much money you used to have. Besides, we have all sorts of offers on the table. I really didn't expect a Nazi and a schoolgirl to be such a hit." He said the last bit quieter, like he was talking to himself.

Bree approached the table. Stood next to Gel. Over the meat. "Oh dear," she said. "You seem to have gotten yourself into such a pickle."

"Lady by the name of Lady," Raymond called across, "has pushed five hundred on the table for the full story."

Bree turned away from the meat and went to the

end of the table and looked up into the camera. "This," she said, "is the waste of space that I dumped last week because he was a slovenly pig, who wouldn't do anything for me, and just wanted me to be his mother and cum rag all wrapped into one. After I dumped his fucking arse, he seemed to have contacted these nice people to have me fucking murdered. And he paid for it."

"She says you can hurt him anyway you please, for a thousand."

Bree smiled into the camera. "Oh, Lady, how can I ever thank you?"

As she rounded back towards the kit, Gel whispered, "Don't kill him, not for that."

Bree winked at her. "Oh, I want this to *last*." She went to the table and, watched by Gel, she took the wallet of acupuncture needles.

"What are you going to do?" Mike demanded, finding his voice again.

Bree assumed he was spending his time looking for escape. But she was sure that Gel and Raymond knew what they were doing. They certainly had done this enough times, according to Gel. She placed the wallet down next to Mike, while he watched wide-eyed.

"Bree," he said. "It's me. You can't do this to me. I wasn't going to do this to you. You have to believe me."

She pulled his pants down, revealing a small skid mark at the back.

"Eww," said Gel, watching. "He's shit."

"No," said Bree. "These one's always look like that." She pulled them down to his knees.

"Jesus. You let this dirty fucker touch you with that?" She pointed to the meat's cock. "You *are* brave."

"Stupid, maybe," she muttered.

Mike was crying. "Please don't. I never did anything to you."

Bree opened the wallet of acupuncture needles and pulled one out. She carefully fingered the end of it. It was like a syringe needle in weight and girth. She leant over him. Looked up into his eyes to see the fear before she touched him. Then she slipped the needle into the skin that surrounded his shaft.

Mike cried out in pain. "No," he said, squirming, which probably didn't help.

Bree pushed it into him, about halfway up the filthy thing. It pushed the skin out the other side, tenting it up, before spearing through it, the needle going in one side and out the other.

Mike crying in fear. "It hurts," he screamed.

Good. Bree looked at him, a little smile.

Gel said, "And the camera."

So she did. She looked into the camera and winked. She bit her lip like she was turned on. Give them something to look at. But she didn't care about that. She only cared about hurting *him*. Then she took another needle, pushing it through his cock criss-cross pattern to the other one.

Mike was making weird inhuman noises. Whimpering.

Begging.

Raymond looked from one screen to the next. Yes. *Yes.* The assembled crowd were digging this. The couple of women seemed engaged. More of the men than usual were clearly aroused by it. He looked over to the girls. Bree told Gel to join in. So she did. Raymond looked back to the camera to make sure it was capturing the scene. The two of them pushing acupuncture needles through his cock at skewed angles. Tiny beads of blood coming out of the pinpricks. He was drooling some from the end of his cock, but watered down, like he'd been turned on before, and the remnant of his pre-cum was mixing with the blood as some of the needles punctured his urethra. He—Mike—*the meat*, was banging his head back and forth on the table. He wasn't shouting for help. Sometimes they did, but he knew better. There was no point in him screaming out. He knew that. He knew where they were. He knew nobody was coming.

"Fingers ... one thousand."

Raymond looked at the name. Alfred. Then to the girls. "Gent by the name of Alfred is asking for fingers."

Gel shot a look back. "Coolio," she said. She looked up to the camera and smiled. "I like fingers," she said. Her hand snaked down between her legs. Touching herself for the audience. Then out as she went to the kit. Got the stubby mallet.

Bree had left his cock alone. By now it looked like something out of a Clive Barker film, and it was getting difficult to find somewhere new to push the needles. She came to his face. "How you holding up, lover boy?" she asked. She gently stretched his fingers out, splaying them. He hadn't paid attention to what Raymond had said.

So he let her.

Bree came up above Mike's head and raised the mallet. Bree left his hand, and the mallet came down hard. The lump smashing into his fingers, breaking three of them, twisting them to impossible angles. Bone shards pushed through the skin, blood spitting out. Mike yowled in pain. His thumb, undamaged, twitching like he was trying to clench a fist. He was going heh-heh-heh as he tried to cry, scream, plead, and beg all at the same time, with what appeared to be little air getting into him.

Bree went to his other hand, splaying it at first, but as soon as Mike realised what she was doing, he curled his fingers to a ball. *No*, he screamed.

Gel shrugged. She brought the mallet up and then crashed it down onto his fist. The bones of the fingers cracking and shattering, digging into his palm, his thumb dislocated, the ball pushing out, but not breaking the skin. Fingernails digging into his flesh. Staying behind after she hit him again—for good measure—and his mess of pulp that used to be his hand unravelled.

Bree slapped him. Trying to shut him up.

"*Death* wants you two to fuck on the, and I quote, *squirming corpse*, for three grand."

Bree looked over at Raymond, his face stony serious, then to Gel. The two of them linked eyes. A spark of fire between them as they shared something. "Nah," said Gel. "Something more squick-tastic."

The two girls giggled.

Raymond quickly looked around the messages. They were flooding in like no other show. The bids getting higher each time. People desperate to see the two of them fucking this guy up. "Okay," he said, "We have eight hundred for his teeth."

Gel shot a look. "Smash or grab?"

Raymond shrugged. It didn't say.

She handed the mallet to Bree. "All you."

Bree held the mallet, and Mike, trying his best to stay in one piece, had clamped his mouth shut, breath reaming in and out of his nose, snot bubbling as it pushed out, weeping down his face. His skin pearly, wet from sweat and sticky with blood spatters from his hands. His head thrashed from side to side, his eyes on Bree's, begging with them. No. Please don't hurt me.

Bree raised the mallet up. "Open wide," she said. "For the choo-choo train." She laughed at him. His silly face, as he gurned some horrified look of terror. "Oh, you," she said. The mallet came down roughly where his teeth should have been. A little hard to tell what with the mouth closed. But it caved in well enough just with the small amount of effort she put in and the weight of the lump.

She lifted it back up. The lower front of his face a divot now, like some shitty golfer had taken a clump of soil out of the immaculately shorn green. Then he opened his mouth and blood chugged from it like a tide carrying little bits of teeth. Bree smirked. She could feel the bile of puke roll a little in her gut, but she just swallowed it away. Fuck him. Fuck all men.

They were all the *fucking same*.

She brought the mallet back up.

"Wait," Gel hissed. She glanced back to Raymond. His head shaking back and forth. It wasn't time.

Bree lowered the lump hammer and turned her look to Raymond. *Come on then*, she thought. Don't leave me hanging.

"Ears," said Raymond, "a grand."

Gel turned to the kit and then back. She held out a spike in one hand. Long thing. Looked like a knitting needle. In the other, a pair of shears. She bobbed them back and forth, like, which one do you want?

Bree took the shears.

Mike was bubbling blood with his mouth, his

face bruised black and purple. The blood that had flowed from his mouth, down his neck, onto the table, clotting and thick. His eyes rolled in his head. Partially gone from this world. Lost in pain and torment. Bree pushed his ear into the mouth of the shears and Gel lined up the knitting needle, and at the same time, Bree removed his ear, just as Gel spiked him through the eardrum.

His left ear—Bree's side—splopped to the table next to him.

Mike thrust his hips forward, arching his back away from the table, up, like he was some masterful man, ejaculating uncontrollably, but it was probably the pain. Then he flopped down to the table. Out. Limp.

Bree went, "Ooh."

Gel looked to Raymond. "We had fifteen on the table for a kill. Lady wants to *see what he's made of*," he said.

She looked at Bree. "You ready for this?"

Bree looked down at him. She was. She wanted to hurt him, sure. But a little bit of her was ready to put him out of his misery. "Sure," she said. Gel was holding out a knife. Looked for anything like a sacrificial dagger.

A glance to Raymond. He was nodding. Eyebrows up like he was surprised she was actually doing it.

She took it from her, and looked at him—peaceful. Probably the most relaxed he'd looked for months. Always angry. Arrogant. But no more. She held the knife out. Gently resting it on his torso.

"In at the base of his gut," Gel whispered. "Deep. It's fucking sharp. Drag it up towards his sternum. When you hit that, pull it out, and we drag him open.

Let the world see. Okay?"

Bree nodded, almost like she wasn't listening, but she was. The dagger went in. Easier than she expected it too. She pushed it down and the stench of piss rose, yellow liquid, dark in colour bloomed in the wound like a puddle forming from below.

"That's okay," Gel said, encouraging her.

Then she pulled the dagger up. The stink of shit when it clipped the bowel. Up. She felt some resistance, but sawed her way through it. Up until she reached the bone. The gash in his body slicked with blood, bits of inside pulled through it before the dagger cleaved through them. Intestines pulsating, bits of last night's food pushed out onto his warm flesh. She was shaking. The thought of killing him, a relief, almost, but she was suddenly very scared.

She was scared of being caught.

But below that, there was a vibration. Some excitement. Something awoken in her, doing this. Vengeance. Revenge without remorse, waiting to bubble over and take every doubt she had. She felt ... stronger.

Gel took the knife from her hand seeing her hesitation and then pushed her fingers into the gaping wound. She looked to Bree and cleared her throat. Snapped back to it, Bree did the same and the two of them pulled the wound open.

"Nice," Raymond chipped in from the screen. "Good job."

Bree looked down into the hole in Mike. His insides moved like they were alive independent of him. His intestines throbbed, and other things, things she didn't recognise slipped together.

"She says you have to finish it."

Bree looked across to Raymond, the smell of

Mike getting in her nose. "No problem." Then she reached inside him. Into his gash and she started to pull his insides out, tearing them away from his body like an animal. The intestines spilling out like sausages, she pulled organs out, away from their housing, muscles and tendons useless against her pulling, yanking, she growled, angered. Every step made against her in life. Him. Work. Fucking men. All of it being torn out of her as his guts were him. She discarded each handful to the side, bits of the meat, slapping wetly to the floor, until she slowed. Air huffing in and out of her. Blood slicked over her, her school uniform. Her skin. The table a mess of gore and fluid. She looked up to Gel, who was still standing there, holding the other side of him open. Her mouth shut, but her eyes wide. "Too much?" Bree said. She glanced down to the meat's lung. Only one still in place. The other pushed to the side and long deflated. It wasn't working either way. "I finished it."

Raymond closed off the room. He was grinning. They'd taken a shit ton of cash just from the show alone, along with the money from the meat and now more from Bree. The two of them were still standing over the corpse. Talking quietly among themselves.

    He was subconsciously pulling the cables from the laptops already, payments in. The fucking clients had loved seeing the two of them doing it. He shook his head, absently, as he watched them while he packed. He should have thought of it before. Getting another hot girl to join Gel. It was a recipe for success. Clearly.

Chapter 25

Gel pulled her top off, discarding it to the floor, picking up the water and starting to wash the blood from herself. It was mostly over her hands and face. Splashes, and spits. Her uniform had caught most of it. She pulled at the short skirt. Her fingers going through the stockings. Didn't matter. They usually went straight in the trash after washing anyway. She cleared her throat. "Hurry hurry," she said.

Bree glanced at her. She was gently caressing her hands, almost smooshing the blood into her skin like lotion. "Yeah," she said.

"So, uh … you wanna a lift home?"

Bree nodded.

Gel thrust her water at the woman. "Here." She was in a daze. Not really a surprise. What *was* a surprise was that she hadn't puked. Gel barfed fucking everywhere after first show she did.

Bree took the water. "You were going to kill me," she said, quietly.

"*Were*, being the operative word. Look, it was nothing personal. We needed the money, okay. And you're fine now." She flashed her a smile. Standing naked, she took the water back, as Bree didn't seem to know what to do with it, splashing it down her legs, getting the specks of the meat from her. Passed the water back, and pulled a towel from the bag. "You should move," she said, drying herself down.

Bree looked at her for a second, and then it seemed to click. She put the water to the side and started to pull the school uniform off herself like it was burning her. "Fuck," she said.

Gel could see she was shaking like a leaf suddenly. "Calm yourself," she said. "What's the problem?"

"Problem?" Bree tore the skirt pulling it over her hips. So heavily soaked in Mike's blood she couldn't even see the clasps holding it closed. "I've just murdered my fucking boyfriend."

"Ex," said Gel, coldly. "Him or you," she added. She pushed the soiled uniform into a carrier bag. Big one. Reusable. She dropped it to the floor in front of Bree. "Put your shit in that one." Then she pulled her clean knickers on.

Bree stuffed the bloody clothes into the bag on top of Gel's, huffing half-cries back up, tears on her face. In the blood. "Yeah," she said, quietly. "Paid for the privilege too."

Gel shook her head and stepped into the gap between them. "Look, you did what you had to. He was going to fucking kill you for shits and giggles. Did you see the hard-on he got looking at you? Ready to hack you up?"

"He said he couldn't." Bree looked Gel in the eyes.

"Then we would have just had to kill you both." She shrugged. Reached up and touched the tears on her face, brushing them into the blood of the meat, and off, away. "You did good. Survival. That means a lot."

Raymond walked in, laptops piled in his arms. He looked at Gel wearing nothing but a pair of panties, and Bree, naked. "Oi, oi," he muttered. "Save it for the camera." Then he continued straight through without saying another word.

Bree snorted a laugh. Watched him leave.

"That's better," Gel said. "You just gotta remember that this is all done now. You can go on like it didn't happen. Just keep your mouth shut when the police inevitably find the corpse." She dropped her head to the side. "Or not." There were still a few bodies out there that had never made the news, and she assumed that they had never been found.

Bree nodded, washing the blood from her hands.

Gel continued to dress, and then stuffed all the soiled clothes in bags into a backpack. She swung it on her shoulder as Raymond crossed back onto the set for more stuff.

Bree washed, watching Gel and Raymond cleaning up. They were almost military about it. Like they'd done it a thousand times. By the time she was ready and dressed, the car was packed. Gel waved her out to it, while Raymond took one last look around.

"Done and done," she said as they got in the car. Gel opened the glove box and pulled out a takeout menu.

Bree thought it was a bit late to be ordering food, and besides, her gut hadn't stopped rolling since the camera's had. Then Gel started doing a line of something off it, and that made more sense. She looked at the sky. It was that time of the morning where the sun was about to breach the horizon and there was this surreal orange glow that appeared to come from the landline. Gel offered the menu forward, and Bree just shook her head. No. And thank you. Then Raymond came from the building and hurried over to the car. Jumped in.

"All clear," he said.

Engine on, and they were away.

"So, you just leave the body behind?" Bree asked.

"Sure," Raymond said. He was in good spirits. "What's the point in dragging the evidence about with us? The last thing anyone needs is a car full of blood. That's after getting rid of the body. And what are you going to do with it? Dump it in a river? Drop it in a ditch? Nah. Leave it good as." He looked over his shoulder. "Besides, sometimes it takes months for some fucker to find it."

Out onto the main road.

Bree watched out the window. Fucking hell. They weren't far from home. Only a few miles. Sure, she'd had to wait until they got to the main road before she'd spotted it, but hell, talk about shitting where you eat. "You from around here?" she asked.

"Fuck no," Gel replied. "Up north way."

"Why come down here?" She watched the world go by. Raymond driving slow. Careful. It was like being driven by her dad.

"That fucker wanted to pay to party," Raymond said. He glanced back to her again. "It was nothing personal, you know that, right? I'm sorry. It wouldn't have happened if I'd known it was going to pan out like this. Also, you were real harsh in that email you sent him and I thought you were going to be a stone cold bitch. But I like you. We just needed the money." He straightened himself back in the seat and pulled the car over, having drifted out to the next lane while he wasn't paying attention.

Then the lights on the police car behind them flashed.

Raymond looked in the mirror. "Fuck."

Gel already had her hand on his knee. "It's fine," she said. "We all just act natural." She shot a look over to Bree. Bree had lost all the colour in her flesh. She looked worse than the meat did.

Raymond was already pulling the car over into the side. "Be cool," he said, possibly more to himself than anyone else. Watching as the door of the police car opened. Guy got out. There was another in there. Sitting, waiting. Great. This was just dandy. What a fucking way to end the most profitable night ever.

The copper knocked on Raymond's window and he brought it down. "Problem, officer?" he asked, buttery smile.

He leant down. "You were driving a little haphazardly sir. Had a drink tonight?"

Raymond glanced to the sun, now up. Still early, no real cars on the road. Who the fuck would be drunk at this time? "No, sir-ee." Fuck. That sounded stupid. Hold it together.

The copper looked around the inside of the car. Two younger women. Everyone looked fucking exhausted. "Been partying?"

Fucker was fishing for an excuse to get his ticket book out.

"Not at all, officer." Raymond remained calm. Everything would be fine as long as he didn't open the boot. The smell of the blood, maybe. It might be all right, as long as he didn't start fishing through bags.

"Not yet," Gel said. She laid a cheeky wink on the copper. He didn't seem enthused.

"And where are we heading?"

"My place," Bree said. She leant forward and put her hand over the seat, onto Raymond's torso, down. Sexy. She felt him tense. Wasn't expecting it. She smiled at the copper. "Look, I would offer for you to join us, but four's a crowd, I heard."

"Maybe it's not," Gel added. She turned in her seat and looked through the back window. "Hmm. But maybe five." Attention back on the copper. "If you could blow off your partner, maybe?" She giggled, hand snaked down into Raymond's lap. "Blow off," she echoed. "I promise we'll behave until we get home, Sir."

The fucking guy had turned crimson red. He looked at the hands on Raymond. His face burning with jealousy and possible embarrassment. Not as much as Raymond, though, who seemed to be joining him in the beet club. "You need to be more careful," he said. "I'm going to let you go this time, but I'll be watching." He tapped the side of his head.

"Ooh," Bree whispered. "He likes to watch."

The copper cleared his throat and grunted something unintelligible, before striding back to the car.

Bree watched him go before unfolding herself from the Raymond and the car seat. "Cunting hell and motherfuckers," she said. Her heart was hammering in her chest. "Piss on a stick."

Raymond started the car. "Nice work, girls."

Gel looked in the rear view on her side as they pulled out. "Straight and slow baby, they're following us."

Raymond took the car to five below the speed limit and stayed straight in the lane. Taking the first turn off to the town. "What's the easiest way back to your place?" Raymond asked.

"They're following," Gel said.

"Christ." Bree looked back to them. Gel was right. They'd taken the turn into the town. Could be a coincidence. She started reeling off the directions back to her place. Each time they turned, the panda car following turned.

Until they were in her road. "There," she said. "Space out the front."

The fuckers were still there, following them home.

Raymond pulled up outside the building.

"Everybody out," Bree said. "Party in mine." She was in self-preservation mode. No way was she going to get off if the truth outed. *My ex set me up to be murdered on the dark web by these two dead broke, but lovely people, and he couldn't do it, so I did.* Going down for life. Without doubt. She opened the door and got out. Almost falling into Raymond's arms. Gel coming around the car. One each side of him. Put a show on for the boys in blue.

Bree was all over him. She rounded to Gel as they got to the door and kissed her, too. Then opened the building up and in. The three of them in the hallway, hurrying to the front door and in.

Bree left them to their own devices as she rounded the flat to the bathroom and peeked out the window. She saw the police car pulling around in a circle and leaving. Felt the relief wash over her like a hot shower. She glanced at the shower. Yeah. She needed a proper wash. Looking at her fingers, there was dried blood all caked under her nails. She could see Mike's blood on her. Lucky the police had pulled them over in the early morning light.

She left the bedroom. Gel and Raymond standing anxious in the hall, by the front door. "They're gone," she said. "But I think you should hang here, at least for a little while." She held the door to the living room open for them. "Can't have you bumping straight into them, now, can we?"

Raymond looked at Gel a little unsure, and the

look morphed over to Bree. She smiled as best she could. As the adrenaline of everything that had happened started to run down, she was clamming up. Shaking. She didn't know these people. They weren't her friends. They were going to kill her only hours ago.

She eyed Raymond as the two of them shuffled uncomfortably forward, into the living room and plopping down on the sofa.

She'd let them into her house. She was a loose end, wasn't she? They were going to fuck her up. Skin her alive. Chop her head off and have weird sex with it. "Coffee?" she asked. A slight smile.

"Sure," Gel replied. She smiled back.

Bree went to the kitchen like she had fucking people over for fucking afternoon tea and started making drinks. Didn't ask how they took it. Fuck that. They were getting white with sugar. Surely that was what people drunk these days after a hard night carving up their ex boyfriends in abandoned farms in the middle nowhere. But rather close to the house. Fuck. She was going to be a suspect, wasn't she?

No. It didn't matter.

She was going to be the second corpse. She shivered, pouring the water into the mugs and carrying them through. What the fuck was she doing? *Run bitch, run*. She put the coffee down on the table in front of the sofa and then sat with the third one. She held it, the smell of the coffee somehow warming.

And she wanted a shower.

"We've been talking," Raymond said.

This was it. We've been talking about how we're going to kill you. Have sex with you while you're still warm. Mind if we set up the cameras? "Go on," she said. There was a little round of applause from the audience in the back of her head, congratulating her at taking her impending violent death so well.

"We took a good haul tonight," he continued. Picked up his coffee. Held it with a little pinky sticking out.

She ignored it. Focus on the mad dog killer.

"We were wondering if we could proposition you."

He looked nervous. What? You're going to *ask* to fuck me up? Go for it. What options do I have with you sitting in my living room drinking my coffee?

"Would you be interested in working with us again?"

"Huh?" Bree stared at him.

"We'd pay you, of course," Gel cut in.

Bree looked from him to her. What? What now? Work for them? "You mean …" she let the words hang there, hoping that one of them would fill in the blanks. Which was all of it.

"We want you to do what you did today, but again. Come in with us. Dress up. Play for the camera."

Gel had said it like it was a sleep over. "Yeah," she said, absently. Uh-oh. Her brain was packing up and taking a holiday. "What?"

"Join us," Raymond said.

Then her head filled with the Evil Dead chant. *Join us*. "You want me to kill people for money?"

Raymond smiled and nodded. Sipped his coffee. Like it was just any other question. Want to come for a picnic at the weekend? Want to watch the new James Bond movie on TV? Want to cut up a stranger for money? "Okay," she said. Sure. Whatever.

Still. She did need a new job.

"I'm gonna need to think about it." She cracked a half smile at the two crazy people drinking her coffee.

"You did well today," Raymond continued with the hard sell. "Both on and off the camera. You rocked the on-camera stuff. Cool as a cucumber in front of that copper. If we were to roll the same as we did tonight, we can probably pay you … I don't know … in the region of five grand a show."

Bree stared at him.

And a-what now?

Chapter 26

"I've got your ... rabbits." Raymond shook his head. Stupid fucking rabbits. Stupid fucking Luca. The dots on the chat window ran, bobbing up and down as he typed.

Twenty five.

Raymond stared at it for a second. No. No, it was *fifteen*. "Fifteen."

Interest, my little friend.

Fuck. This wasn't going to go away, was it? He looked over the screen of the laptop to Gel, sleeping on the sofa. Her feet up. The TV playing some rank horror film, the sound down, all but muted. Raymond had never had the stomach to watch horror flicks. More of a book man, himself. He looked back to the laptop screen. Fuck Luca. "You're getting the fifteen I owe you."

I can take the interest out on your woman, if you prefer.

His eyes flicking to her body, prone. Shallow breaths. She'd taken something to help her sleep. Which was just as well, because he could imagine what his face must be saying at that moment. "You're a fucker."

Oh yes.

"You'll have to wait." He closed the lid of the laptop and picked up his phone. Opened up his messaging there. Bree. "You ready if we are?" He reopened the laptop and started scouting the areas around the east of the country, just north of the smoke. He needed to factor in Bree for now. Once she was settled, if she was going to continue on with them, then she could ferry herself to and from the sets, but until that time, she'd have to travel with them. Somewhere around London suited. Close enough to get to her, the set, back again, and not be working for twenty hours straight.

There was an abandoned airport. That would do nicely. He pushed himself from the chair and went to the kitchen. Made a sandwich.

Phone buzzed. *That was quick,* she messaged. *Thought it was going to be a couple of weeks.* She ended the message with a smiley face. No sense in giving her the low down on Luca. She wasn't involved in that, and there was no reason for her to be. Ever.

N o w   S t r e a m i n g

"The fingers," Raymond said. "Eight hundred." He raised his eyebrows as he said it.

Gel glanced to Bree, Bree glanced to the meat.

"No," the meat scream-whimpered. "Fucking hell for the love of God."

Bree shrugged. Cash was cash. She turned and looked at the kit. She fingered the shears. They were cool, but then so was the hatchet. And she really didn't get to use the hatchet that much. She picked it up and felt the weight. Nice. Turned back to Gel.

"Cool," she said over the screams of the meat. She was writhing. Naked. Hot. They'd barely even touched her yet. It was that time of the show, you know, where it was still sexy. Before the room smelled like blood and butchery and there was twitching.

Bree straightened the meat's hand out, stroking it like a lover.

"Mind your fingers," Gel said to Bree. "Unwieldy that thing is. Don't want to cut yourself." Her eyes flicked to the meat, and she giggled embarrassingly. "Yeah," she said. "*Sorry.*"

Then she clamped her fingers shut, stopping Bree from managing to get a nice clean swing.

"I'll give you anything." The meat was crying like a cry-face baby. It made her less pretty. Her makeup was striped on the left hand side of her face, like the tears only came from that side. She had sparkly shit—fucking glitter—in it that had run down, onto her lips. Made her look like a horror movie final girl.

"But I only want your fingers," Bree barked, theatrically. She had her own SS costume now and she was really quite getting into it. The two of them *Ilsa*-ing it up. The meat held a fist now. Both hands. But it wasn't going to stop Bree. Not at all. She showed the hatchet to the meat, and then to the camera. She muttered something sexual, under her breath, nothing more than grunts to the mic, before turning back to the meat. "Would you fuck the axe. Axe in the axe wound?" she asked. The look on the meat's face was a tormenting gurn of horror, but she was nodding. Yes. She would fuck the axe if it meant she could live. Bree teased her with it, rubbing the handle of the thing to the meat's cunt. "You like that?" Again the meat nodded.

She shook her head, glancing to Gel as she wandered from the shot.

Gel went to Raymond sliding off screen. She leant in, whispering, "What the fuck have we unleashed?" with a half laugh.

Raymond was shaking his head. "I don't fucking know, but look at them." He jabbed his finger to the screen.

Gel leant over. Nearly half of them were getting off to it. The crowd was more mixed with men and women, and they seemed largely to be an older crowd. "They really dig this shit?"

Raymond nodded. "Looks like we found the Gen-X kink."

Gel laughed, covering her mouth, not wanting to

get on the mics. She glanced back to Bree.

Bree raised the hatchet. "Open wide, or it'll hurt even worse." She even had a faux German accent on. But the meat did not open their hand, it remaining a fist.

Oh well.

Bree slammed the hatchet down, just in the general vicinity of the hand. If she wasn't going to open it, then it didn't matter how accurate she was, was it?

The blade of the axe crashed down into the centre of the meat's hand, chunking straight through the fingers and digging deep into the palm. The ends of the four fingers pinging away like roughly chopped carrot ends, to the floor. The axe head stopping, penetrating deep into her hand, but not quite cutting it in two. She screamed, screamed the fucking airport down. "Oh, shush," barked Bree. Yanking the blade from the hand, she raised it again. Little more carefully aimed this time, she slammed it down again, taking the rest of the hand. The hatchet through to the table beneath, the blood fired quickly from the hand, but there was no major artery there and after the initial spurt, it quickly slowed to a dribble, a drool. Then the meat blacked out.

"Shit," Gel said, coming up beside her. She pulled the smelling salts out and started to wave them under her nose. "It's just shock," she continued. She looked down at the hand. "Good job," she said.

Bree was running the tips of her fingers through the blood, sticky on the blade, so the camera could see. Enjoying it. Letting them see her gain some sort of acted out sexual gratification.

The meat screamed awake, again. Yelled out the word, "Help," then her head banged back on the table.

Bree looked at her, and smiled, genuinely, then back to Raymond. Eyebrows up.

"We have fifteen on the table for you to fuck her with the axe, as suggested."

"Jesus," Gel whispered. "That's a kill."

"I know, but fifteen. And we get to finish early."

"True." She looked at Bree, still holding the axe. "Who was it that asked?" she asked, fingering the blade.

"Woman called Fee."

Bree nodded. Something inside had already decided that yes, she would do it, but not for a man. Not this time. So she leant over the meat. "You get to put on a fuck show," she said. A smile. "After all."

The meat was nodding, like she didn't understand. "Yes," she croaked, hoarse. "A fuck show." Her words were weak. The *handjob* had taken some out of her.

Bree smiled, dipped in gently, and kissed her on the lips. Slow. For the camera. Then she turned and pushed the blade of the axe, up against the meat's meat. The meat even did her best to open her legs. Let her. She was delirious from pain and blood loss. Bree pushed the stick of the axe against her vagina and the meat weakly ground down.

Bree stopped, pulled the axe away. She felt her stomach turn.

Oh god. She didn't want to puke.

Not on camera. Not when this was worth so much money.

Gel was holding out her hand. She didn't say anything. She was just waiting for the axe. Must have been able to see it in Bree eyes. So she passed it to her.

Gel took the axe. Looked into the camera.

"Double team," she said, a high pitched giggle. Then to the meat. "Getting fucked by both the bad bitches, aye?" She turned on the meat and brought the axe to her, where Bree had it, but she pushed harder, sinking the axe head into her flesh. The meat screamed out that she was doing it too hard, then the penny seemed to drop and she tried to squirm away, but Gel was hard, the sticky wet axe head, cutting into her flesh, fresh blood coming to join the older. Hot on cold.

Then the axe came out. Up. She swung it down and cleaved it into the meat. She shrieked out in pain and then suddenly silenced. The axehead impaled in her. Gel pulled it out, and blood and viscera chugged forward, out onto the table like afterbirth. The axe the baby. Gel smiled at it, deranged, and then stabbed it into the meat again.

Bree backed away a little. She was weakening, had a headache that had started in the back of her throat and moved upwards.

Gel hacked at the meat a couple more times, before stopping and bowing at the camera. "We'll be back," she said. "Sooner than you expect."

That was a bit of a blow out, but the cold hard cash was good. They'd rolled nearly twenty. Enough with what they had to fuck off Luca, and pay Bree. Maybe that would be the end of it? Raymond closed the room down and glanced over to the girls. Bree didn't look too well. Gel was already cleaning down the axe, ready to re-kit it.

"Don't do that again," Gel said.

"What?" Bree asked. She had a rag in her hand and was patting off the beads of sweat with it.

"Kissing the meat. They get bitey sometimes,

yeah?"

Shit. Bree hadn't thought of that. "Yeah," she replied, quietly. "Christ."

"You don't want to lose that fucking smile, do you?" Gel pushed the axe back in the kit. Left the room, beckoning Bree to follow. The two of them headed into the next room. Gel pulling her uniform off. "Did good tonight. But when we turn a quick one, usually half the audience haven't gotten enough. It's like edging them, right? So we run another room quickly and they're ready to put their hands in their pockets real quick. Blow their load." She opened a bottle of water, took a swig, and then started to wash her chest down. The meat had squirted into the opening of her top. Blood spittle on her breasts. Bree was watching her. "What?"

Bree stopped staring, "Sorry," she said, absently. She pulled her uniform open. Took her own bottle and started to wash off her hands.

"Hands last," Gel said. "Where's your head at?"

Bree shivered. "I don't know. Doing a ... girl. It's different."

"They're all different, babe." Gel took her hand. She was shaking. "If you can't do this, then we can part ways. If Raymond thinks that we should be using a second, it doesn't have to be you. I mean, we'd have to kill you." She paused for a second, waiting as Bree's eyes widened, "I'm joking," she snapped. "You got in deep enough that I know our secret is safe." She dropped Bree's hand. "Besides," she said, turning away, "this isn't the movies. You can't just demand immunity if you turn us in." She pulled her skirt off.

Raymond came in. Completely ignored their state of undress. Had the cameras. "I'm just putting this lot in the car," he said, passing.

"We'll do another," Gel said. "But Bree would like boys."

Raymond glanced at Bree and shrugged. Left.

Gel turned her attention back to cleaning herself up. "See. No questions asked."

Chapter 27

"I've made the transfer," Raymond said in the chat window. It had emptied them out, but with another job coming almost immediately he was happy to break the bank, if only for a few days. Luca didn't respond immediately. He was probably checking.

Raymond looked over to Bree. She was laying half across the sofa. Had a blanket over her. She was asleep but it was fitful. She was having nightmares about something. Which was probably understandable. Hell, he'd had nightmares for months when they started doing this shit.

He could see a light at the end of the tunnel now though. He'd just get another couple of jobs done with Gel and Bree, get enough money together and the two of them would skip the country. Somewhere Luca—people *like* Luca—had no reach. Couldn't infect Gel, not while she was in rehab. Cold turkey.

That would be the end of it.

It's not enough.

Raymond looked at the reply. Cunt. That sealed his suspicion in a heart shaped envelope though. It was never going to be enough, was it? Luca was going to spend forever blackmailing money out of them.

"It's all you're getting," he typed. Pressed enter. He stared at the cursor. Luca was replying. He was going to have to get moving, then. Raymond shut the laptop without waiting for him to finish, and looked at the room. Nothing in particular. Had a lot going on in his head at that moment.

His eyes crossed the door and Gel was standing there, watching him. She had that cute little smile on her face. She'd taken something, no doubt. She crept to the back of the sofa and looked over it to Bree.

They'd decided that she should just go back to theirs. In for everything, together now, rather than take the extra risk to take her home and then go and pick her up again, probably in less than forty-eight hours.

Gel pointed at him, then curled her finger over, beckoning him over. Raymond pushed the laptop quietly onto the coffee table, his eyes on Bree, making sure he didn't wake her. Then he stood. Gel had parted her dressing gown. Naked beneath.

She backed to the door, still drawing him forward, like a cartoon rabbit lured by smell, unable to even consider stopping himself. Rounding the sofa out into the hall. Gel was disappearing into the bedroom, arse out. The gown heaped on the hallway floor where she'd let it drop from her.

Raymond followed to the bedroom. Closed the door quietly. She was already on the bed. Laying on her side facing the door. Hand under the side of her head. One knee up. Everything on show. Raymond's body reacted. He pulled his shirt up, over his head. Noticed that it was getting a little tighter on the chest, and he hadn't been working out. He needed to take care of that. South of France. That would be perfect.

He dropped his jeans off, cock already hard, just having her there on the bed waiting. He slipped onto the sheets as she rolled to her back, legs apart, welcoming him in. He crawled in, between her. Could smell her sex. Almost made him stop and spend a little time there, but he ached for her. He rolled his tongue over her nipples, circling her areola, then continued up, his face close to hers, as his cock probed her. Looking for an entrance.

"You want me to ask Bree to join us?" she whispered. "We could both suck your cock at the same time." Her eyes flickered down. "It's certainly big enough."

Raymond grinned and shook his head. He'd never want that. Never wanted anything or anyone else, not since he'd met her. He slipped up, inside her, and she heaved in air, let out a little whine of satisfaction.

That was all he wanted.

Bree opened her eyes to the sound of a loud crack. Sounded like a gunshot. Fuck. She almost fell from the sofa, in an instant, wondering where she was. Gel's place. Raymond. That was right. She pushed herself up to sit. Shit. Maybe it was a dream. Her head throbbed. She got to her feet. Looked down herself. She didn't have a change of clothes, and Gel's clothes only sort of fit her. She would have brought an overnight if she'd known. Up, she went to the door and listened. She looked down the hallway. Doorway at the end was closed. There was the front door. She blinked the sleep away, and waited. There was something coming from the closed door.

Then a light call. Not quite a scream, but enough for her to know what was going on down there. She walked between the doors to the kitchen, and went in. It was a small square little thing, table for two in the middle. She poured a glass of tap water, and sat, pushing the door closed, so as not to disturb the lovebirds. She pulled her phone. Had another message from Leslie. Jesus. When was she going to get it that they weren't going to be outside work friends?

She still hadn't picked up her bag, though. So she probably should send her a message back.

Then the kitchen door opened. Raymond. Had a gown on. Hanging open. Hard cock underneath. Naked. He looked at Bree. Bree looked at his cock. "Fucking hell," Raymond snapped, pulling the gown closed, "Shit. Sorry. I thought you were still asleep."

He clearly wasn't used to having house guests.

Bree grinned. "I saw nothing," she said, focussing down on her water. Only looking back once he'd moved—suitably embarrassed—to the fridge. Silly boy. Boy. He was older than she was, and Gel. Possibly both of them put together. He pulled a bottle of wine from the fridge and took a couple of glasses. Made some uncomfortable sounds and then left, closing the door behind himself.

Bree heard him mutter, "For Christ's sake," to himself as he returned to the bedroom.

She giggled. Closed her eyes. She could see the meat. There behind her eyelids. Opened them again, quickly. Balls. She wasn't cut out for this, was she? At least, not against women. Shit. She was hoping that she was going to make bank on this, not worry about having a real job for a while.

Not got the stomach for it, she supposed.

She closed her eyes again, and pushed the visage of the meat to one side. Raymond had refused to tell her the girl's real name. He said that it would be easier that way. She supposed he was right. Probably.

Didn't feel easier.

Not at all.

Chapter 28

"One more after this," Raymond said. His eyes on the road, the street flashing passed as he drove towards the city.

Gel's eyes flicked from the screen to him, then out the window. Then back to the screen. She tapped something in.

"How's it coming?" he asked.

She glanced up. "Fine. He's in the bag."

Bree was hanging over the back of Gel's seat, watching the transaction go down. It *was* a transaction. Raymond had no doubt about that. Payment with flesh. Just not the way the mark thought. He thought he was getting fucked, and oh, he was *so* getting fucked. Raymond looked over to the other side of the motorway. Accident. Blue flashing lights. Must have been pretty bad. He returned his attention back to the road. Going over the speed limit. They were late to get to the set.

Needed to set up and get the meat.

"Oh, god," Bree blurted.

Raymond looked. "What?" The two of them hunched over the phone.

"He sent a ... you know," Gel said, half giggling. "Fucking peeny."

"Pervert," Raymond growled. Fucking kids these days. It was all dick pics and ... and ... whatever Gel sent. Probably had a name like *vagina texts*. No. That was shit. Something like that but better.

"You're not jel, are you?"

Raymond looked over to Gel putting on stupid puppy dog eyes. "Oh, fuck off," he said, a massive grin. "Jealous. Pfft."

The two girls started laughing and got back to laying it on the poor schmuck. Guy was doomed. Fuck it, most people who spoke to Gel were doomed. You couldn't help but fall in love with her. Raymond indicated and pulled across three lanes for the off ramp, following a chorus of horns. *Losers*.

He slowed, only just maintaining the control needed to take the corner, and then they dropped onto the next motorway. In between the cars. Out to the fast fucking lane. Raymond noticed that Bree sat back and put her seatbelt back on. Gel looked over her shoulder. "It's okay, he's quite a good driver when he wants to be." She shot Bree a grin. Then her attention came to him. "Far?"

"Twenty minutes." Raymond took them back across the lanes to the other side and off at the next junction. Slowing, this time, leaving the motorway properly. He slipped the car into the left at the traffic lights. Onto the roundabout. Off at the business park. Sunday night. The warehouse he had his eye on was fucking derelict anyway, right on the far end of the estate, away from most of the working factories, but even better, on a Sunday night. There weren't going to be any interruptions.

Raymond took the car down, onto the estate. The first thing he saw was a couple of burned out buildings. Nice place. As the road merged with the estate, there were a couple of hookers on the path, trying to flag down some john. Here. On the edge of an industrial estate. Wow. He drove on, ignoring them.

"They a problem?" Bree asked.

Raymond shook his head. He was preoccupied, making sure the factories were as empty as he hoped they would be.

And, it seemed they were.

He took a couple of turns. The place was a maze. Then out to the rear of it. The factories thinned, until there were barely any buildings at all. Just chain link fences and burned out motors. Nothing to see for miles. He smiled. Pulled the car out to the lone standing building. He killed the lights and got out. Made a shushing gesture to the girls. Then he went to the building. Listened.

He had to be careful now. All this was rushed. He hadn't had time to properly set up a location for the set. He also hadn't touched base with Luca, and he was sure that was going to cause him a problem if he let it.

A quick scout around and then, when he was satisfied, he got Gel's attention to help him set up.

He made sure they'd seen, then he went looking for a table or something. Up a flight of metal stairs on the main factory floor he found a chair, but not much else. "Shit," he mumbled to himself. He lugged it down the stairs, walking backwards, so he could bang the chair down a couple of steps at a time. Thing weighed a ton. He got to the bottom to find the two girls standing and watching. "What?" he grunted.

"They do prisoner executions down here or what?" Gel said with a grin.

Raymond looked at the chair. He could see her point. It was mostly made of wood, and had a tall back to it, like a throne, or an electric chair. Weird. It wasn't *that* surprising, to be honest. He was used to finding all sorts of shit in these places. They were trespassing in buildings that had been empty for some time—years some of them.

He dragged the chair to a good spot. Sat in it and looked around. Yeah. That would do. There were plenty of camera spots available. He went and tested the electric. Fucking hell. Didn't work.

Then out to the car and picked up the gen.

The three of them unloaded the car and set up. Sharp and quick.

When they were three-quarters done, Raymond raised his eyebrows at Gel, taking her attention. "Time?" he asked.

"Time," she said, nodding.

Chapter 29

Why they'd chosen to play them both into this wankers fantasy he didn't know. Sure, most of the time they left the gear unattended when they went to get the meat, but if there were three of them, then Bree could have waited there. But no. Gel and Bree had tied this meat up in threesome circles. So they both had to be there.

It was dangerous.

Stupid, even. All of them out in the open like that. And this fucktard coming out to pick up two sweet chicks in the middle of the evening. The guy was clearly going to be a fuckboy. A show off. He might make a scene, just to get people's attention. Raymond's finger tightened on the steering wheel as he watched the two of them.

Standing on the steps to the library.

Middle of the high street.

There was a middling amount of foot traffic. Not like it was a Friday night or anything. But busy enough. Then he heard the guy. From all the way over there. Fucking hell. He looked over to the left. Guy in a leather jacket. Tall. Chonky. Raymond could tell even from that distance. He was waving and making too much noise. Fucker. Drainpipe jeans wearing stupid peak cap beardy wankface. Raymond drew air into his lungs slowly. A long relaxing breath.

Calm down.

He looked back to Gel and Bree. They were close to each other. Looked like a couple. When they saw him coming they kissed each other. Show on for the horndog. That would be Gel's idea. Again, stupid. She was taking risks. Going to get noticed.

The two of them went to him. Then they were both on him like sugar on a doughnut. The guy looked like he might just fucking explode. Couldn't believe his luck.

Gel raised her phone to her face. That was the signal.

Raymond started the engine and pulled over the road. He slid his window down. "Uber?" he said.

"That was quick," the mark said. Had his arm around Bree's shoulders. Hand in Gel's. Holding onto them, in case if he let go they might disappear. Fulfilling every fantasy in his head. He didn't pay Raymond enough attention to get an answer.

His mind on other things.

The three of them piling in the backseat of the car.

Raymond took the car out, heading straight towards the edge of town. Gel said something about the address to him. All part of the act.

He looked in the mirror. Watched the two of them getting the guy going.

Then Bree stuck him with the needle. He slapped the back of his neck like he'd been stung by a wasp. He said something about the Dulux dog, as he flopped down. The last throes of God knows what, circling in his head before he blacked out.

"I was beginning to think you were enjoying that." Raymond looked in the mirror to see Bree scrapping her tongue with her fingers, trying to get the taste of him off.

Or not, he thought.

Good.

Gel climbed over to the front seat, slipping down onto the fabric. "Fuck that," she said. She took Raymond's hand and pulled it over to her, up her short skirt. "Only for you," she whispered.

He could feel her heat there. She was hot. Excited. It made him feel the same way.

Returning to the estate, the prossies were gone. The whole place, dead. Soon to be deader, he hoped.

Tonight. Maybe a couple more, he told himself. Then they were out.

N o w   S t r e a m i n g

Gel brought the blade up before stabbing it down in the meat's knee. He was sitting in the chair, bound in like it was an electric chair. Naked. With a knife sticking out his leg, the blade slipping between the flesh and the patella. He screamed, deep. He had a husky voice. Which was nice. Shrill screams were really fucking annoying on set. For the camera, she assumed it only mattered depending on what you liked.

He tried to squirm but he was too well restrained for that. His eyes flicking between them. "I can give you anything," he shouted, far too loudly in Gel's opinion. "I know your names."

That was new. Bouncing from begs to threats in the same sentence.

"You don't, I can assure you," Bree said. She was standing behind the meat, waiting for a new instruction.

Raymond looked around the faces. They all seemed really into it at first but it was slowing. A bloke by the name of Jez offered three hundred for the finger nails.

"Three hundred, finger nails," he relayed over to Gel.

She looked up to Bree, hissed, "It doesn't seem worth it. What's wrong with them?" she turned to the kit and took two pairs of pliers, handing one to Bree.

"Fucking hell, please," the meat whined. "I have money. I have things. I can get you drugs. What do you want?"

The two of them ignored it like white noise. You had to, didn't you? If you listen to the lambs as they are slaughtered, you might find you have a heart. Gel flattened his hand out. He was too shit scared to fight back. She grabbed a nail with the nose of the pliers and yanked hard. The finger nail detaching with ease. She was good at it.

He howled when Bree split the nail in half, the broken shards gouging his flesh underneath. Inexperience, that was. Blood dribbling from his fingers. Drooling out to the floor on that side.

"Ouchie," she snapped. Then did pretty much the same thing to the next nail.

He was crying now. Like a child. Grizzle face.

Gel shook her head. It was less fun when the money didn't flow. She looked up to Bree, wondered if they might end up having to put on some sort of fuck show. Just to get the cash. The thought wasn't abhorrent to her, but certainly not something she relished. She focussed back and pulled his thumb nail. Thumb nails hurt no matter how well versed you were on the nail pulling song sheet.

Then a smell rose. Something weird and unpleasant.

Fucker had shit.

"Jesus," Bree blurted, the stench of shit joining the stench of copper and metal. "He's shit."

"No shit," said Gel, she winked at her.

"Heh." Bree put some weight on the back of his hand with hers. Steadied his fingers, before she grabbed the next nail. A quick look told her that Gel could do this without fucking his fingers up. Not something she had so far managed. She yanked. The nail split. The meat screamed. "Shit," she muttered, the smell getting right up her nose.

"Can't we hose him down?"

"Three thousand for the toes," Raymond called over. That was better. Starting to pick up. It seemed that the audience tonight needed some blood to get them going. He looked over. Gel handing a hammer to Bree to smashy-smashy, and she had the shears. Nice. Double team with different implements. A crowd pleaser.

Another request. Love-You-Long-Time, said, "I want to fuck the girls."

Raymond shook his head. Not the first time he'd had sexual propositions for Gel from the audience. One dude offered thirty-eight grand just to get head tied to a table—Red Room style. He even wanted it broadcast. For everyone to see.

Thirty-eight grand. Weird number. Must have been his every penny. Raymond looked at Gel's arse. He understood.

Of course they'd said no. He reached up to block the guy, when the next message came through from him.

"I'll wipe your slate clean."

Raymond held his finger. He looked at the window with the guy's face in. Didn't recognise him. He leant in. Forward. Then his camera glitched. It wasn't a feed. It was a deep fake. "What the fuck," he whispered.

"Good evening Raymond," he said.

Fuck. *Luca*. Instinct told him to block him. Then

he thought about killing off the whole show. Closing the room. But he hesitated. If Luca had tracked them down here, then he would track them down in the next one. "What the fuck do you want?" he typed back.

"I want my money. Or I'll take the girls."

"Fuck you. You had your money."

"You're trying to underpay me. It won't work."

It wasn't true. He had paid him all the money they owed. And stupid amounts more on top. He'd cleaned them out to get rid of this cunt and now he was here. Annoying him in the workplace.

"What's going on?" Gel hissed.

Raymond looked up. They were trying to entertain the audience, having long finished with the meat's feet. One set of toes scattered to the concrete and another smooshed to mash potato. Fuck. He looked back at the screen. Luca was gone. Or at least the fake face he was using. He looked suspiciously around the faces. What if he was more of them? Spoofing himself into more windows.

"One thousand, the cock."

Bree was wiggling it about, hoping to make it hard, but once you'd been the meat for more than a few minutes the chance of getting an erection was small. She should have thought to give him a pill before they started. That still worked, and the audience loved to see a guy with a boner getting his hands cut off.

Among other things.

Gel came at him, with the shears in one hand and a branch saw in the other. "Choices," she hissed in his face.

He made this incomprehensible gargling sound, but to be honest she was quite impressed he was still awake.

Gel grinned at him. "Okie dokie." Then she tossed the shears back into the kit. "Hold him up."

Bree gripped the glans end of his cock and pulled it upwards, stretching it out to its full length. It was slippery where he'd already peed a little. Then Gel hiked up the branch saw. She made a sawing motion for both the meat and the camera, before pushing the teeth of the blade to the skin.

Wee ejected from him, as he lost control. Up like a squirt gun and covering the three of them.

"Cunt," Gel barked, before starting to hack off his cock.

The blood fired from it, quickly mixing with piss as she hit his tubework. The projectile pee stopped, slowing to a drool, and then entirely once Bree was holding his penis in her hand, *unattached*.

She looked at the camera, smiling, and then waved it at the audience, before tossing it to the floor and stamping on it like a cigarette.

Piss and blood flowed with ease from the meat. He was losing consciousness, his eyes rolled back into his head before it began to loll.

"Not long," she said to Raymond.

Raymond scoured the screen. No one was looking for a kill, so he offered it out. "Who's willing to offer the kill? Five thousand?"

It was under price, but fuck it. If he was about to die from his injuries anyway, then he might as well get what he could from it.

"Five thousand, decap." A woman named 69.

Fuck. If he'd known he was going to get a decapitation, he'd have charged more. But those are the breaks.

"Decap," he said. "Finish it."

Gel raised an eyebrow. "Gotcha," she said. A quick look to Bree. "We have to move. This dude is about to bleed out."

Bree nodded. "What do you want me to do?"

"Hold him up by the hair. Head up. Tight as you can. Taking the head is easier when they're laying down—which they usually are. Probably why they've asked for this."

Bree grabbed handfuls of the meat's hair, holding his head up. He was mumbling about something, his mind off, lost somewhere else. Which was fine. No one ever needed to know that two chicks were about to cut their head off. She picked the branch saw from the kit, now sticky with his blood as it cooled on the blade.

She rounded him, making sure she wasn't in the way of the camera, and brought the saw to his neck. "You see," she whispered, "do it higher on the neck and the jugular is deeper. It means the kill is more impressive."

Bree nodded, taking it in.

Then Gel drew the blade back, the skin, thin, tearing under the teeth. She didn't push hard. The kill should look as impressive as it can. The skin parted and the blood oozed out, thick. Then she pushed a little harder as she forced the blade back across his neck. Into the muscles and flesh. Tendons ripping, bloodletting.

He made noises of strangulation and of drowning.

Blood spat from his mouth.

Bree pulled the head harder as he struggled at first, trying to twist. But his mind wasn't there. It was instinctual motion. Panic.

The blade in, further, deeper. The blood glooping out quickly at first, slowing as the blade got to the windpipe, the blood slipping down into him. Unconscious now, drowning in his own blood. Gel yanking the saw back and forth penetrating the spine.

As she got through, the head pulling up easier, the meat inside his neck tearing away with the saw.

The head in Bree's hands. Staring out to the nothing. Juices and fluids running from the neck out, to the corpse beneath, still twitching, headless.

Raymond stopped the show. Closed the room.

"That's it," he said. "We're done." He was already on his feet.

"What's wrong?" Gel asked.

Chapter 30

After packing up the car in record time, they were back on the road. Neither Gel nor Bree was properly clean, but Raymond was spooked. He wanted out. Unwilling to say anything in his hurry to leave.

They'd nearly left one of the laptop cases behind.

His head wasn't in the game.

Gel had stopped him, by the car, as he was getting ready to leave. She'd kissed him. Deep. Lovingly. She'd slowed him down. "Wait," she'd said. "Calm down, and check the set."

Then he'd picked up the last case in there, and they'd left.

"Luca," he said. "He was in the audience. One of the clients."

"Who's Luca?" Bree asked from the back seat.

Gel looked at the takeout menu on her lap. With the line of speed on it. "Fuck," she said. "What the fuck did he want?"

"Who's Luca?" Bree asked, again.

Raymond glanced from the road, over his shoulder at Bree, but didn't answer her. "We need out," he said to Gel. "He can track us. Find us. You know he can. He does it all the time."

Gel was nodding. "Cunt," she whispered.

"Who the *fuck* is Luca?" Bree barked.

Gel leant down and snorted the speed, sitting, sniffing up the remnants, and blinking it away, before she stuffed the menu under Bree's nose, and turned in her seat. "Dude's bad juju. He's a dealer, but a bastard. He says we owe him money, which we don't by the way."

Bree looked at the menu and then listened to Gel telling her what a cunt this guy was. And how dangerous he was. Then she took the menu and snorted whatever was on it.

Made her sneeze.

"He said if he could fuck you two then he'd wipe the slate," Raymond said.

"Then let's do it," Bree said quickly. "Fuck it. It's a quick fuck and you two are free."

Gel was shaking her head. "Luca doesn't work like that. It's a lie. He'd just get us where he wants us. Probably to kill us. Or worse."

"Worse?"

"Keep us." Gel looked at her. "Besides. We couldn't ask you to do that. You have no beef with him."

"I say we do one last show. Tomorrow," Raymond said. He'd been staring out the window silently, watching the night go by. "What do you think, Bree?" he looked at her in the mirror.

"Sure," she said. The world felt weird. "What was that?" she asked.

"Speed. It'll just make everything a little clearer for a while."

"You come back to our place, then?" Raymond asked. "Get everything ready?"

Bree nodded, looking out the window. The lights looked sharper in the distance. The feeling wasn't unpleasant.

"We'll need meat," he said.

Gel already had her phone in her hand. "That's no

problem. I can get a profile set up tonight and we can—"

"Hold on that," Bree said. She leant forward between the two seats. "I'm guessing this last show is the *last-last* show?"

"Yeah. We'll be jumping ship. Leaving the country."

"You get a ticket for me?" She smiled. "I know a meat sack we can use."

Chapter 31

Bree slept hard. That *speed* that she had taken was cool and all, but the come down was shit. She should probably stay off it. Pulling her eyes open, she saw there were suitcases packed on the floor in the corner.

The two of them readying to leave. For good.

She was going to go with them. Use them as an alibi, but she was going to come back in a month or two. There was no way she wanted to live in the South of France. There were too many French people there.

"You're awake," Gel said, dropping a bag down. "When do you want to head to your place? Raymond said he'd take you anytime."

"Whenever."

"You have the address for the meat already?"

"Yeah. I do." She smiled up at Gel. "Coffee?" she asked, pushing herself from the sofa.

"It's already on. Yes, please." Gel smiled, left the room.

Bree went to the kitchen. She could hear Raymond and Gel talking as they packed. Raymond sounded stressed. He kept saying things about looking after her, and wishing he could just kill Luca.

Gel was telling him that all the while Luca had been up his arse, killing him would have just put a target in Raymond's head. It was going to be obvious it was him.

Placating him.

Bree poured three coffees. If Luca was this uber cunt then surely it wouldn't be obvious who killed him? He must have a pile of enemies? Bree shook her head. But, in all fairness, what did she know? She dropped two sugar cubes in hers. She felt half asleep and drowsy.

"How you doing?" Raymond walked in, Gel holding hands with him. The two of them took their coffees, and the three of them sat around the table.

"Fine. I just feel bad that you two have got to leave." She shrugged. These were the best people she had come to know. In a *long* fucking time.

"You never know," Gel said. "You might enjoy it down there. You might want to stay."

"Will you still be working?"

Raymond dropped his head to the side. "We will, but I think a change of direction will be coming up. I don't really want to end up in a French prison for forty years. I don't even know if they have the death penalty."

Bree nodded. "What's the plan then?"

Raymond snorted a laugh. "Someone keeps telling me that we should start an OnlyFans thing. Fuck on camera for money."

Bree shrugged, slowly. "You have done worse."

The three of them laughed.

"Your old stomping ground," Raymond said, pulling up to the garage block. Old thing. Left to rot on the edge of town. Half of them were burnt out and fucked. The other half still standing, but dank and rotten. Graffiti up the walls that may have been there since before they were abandoned, maybe after.

Gel looked out the window. "Bit close to the town aren't we?"

Bree eyed the fields out to the left, the garages and then looked down, back to the main road. "It's fine. No one comes out here now. Not since the owner of the land torched the buildings. Insurance job, you know? Anyway. He got banged up and some kid was raped here. Since then not even the little shits come down here. It's like it's a pariah. We'll be fine. Gonna need the generator though."

Raymond was already half out the car. "Give me a sec." He strode straight past the burned out buildings. You could already see there was no one in there lurking. The garages, some double, some single, a couple of them even had two floors, held a stink of old soot. Burned out years ago, but these sorts of buildings held on to the scent. That, and he probably used something stupid as the accelerant. Petrol was always the choice of the amateur. Easy to pick up. Didn't need Sherlock Holmes to know it was arson.

He crossed to the ones that hadn't been touched by fire. Looked into the first two he came to. Both single storey garages, with fucked up shutters. Broken open. Beer cans on the floor. Little burn piles where kids had come down here, made a bonfire and done weed. Got pissed. Fucked.

The third was a two storey job. Little workshop feel to it. He went in. The ground floor was just a hollow shell. He listened. The building creaked a little, like it was trying to tell him something. The door at the back, hanging from its hinges. The stairs to the second floor, wooden. He crept up, making sure he wasn't going to fall through. Second floor had a shitter. Wasn't plumbed into anything. Maybe had one of those caravan setups where you had to take your pot of shit and dispose of it somewhere. Nice. All the mod-cons. But that bit wasn't attached anymore. It was just a shitter sitting in the corner of the room.

He went back down to the car. Hurried over to Gel. "Okay. We'll use that one. I'm going to look around for a chair or something. You start getting things ready. We'll have the set on the ground floor, changing room upstairs."

Gel grinned, a nod to him, then flashed her smile back to Bree. "Action," she said, pushing the door open.

Chapter 32

He didn't like leaving Gel at the set, getting things ready. Not one little bit. She could look after herself, sure, but he would have rather had her with him. He glanced to Bree in the passenger seat. Left her behind instead. But that wasn't how this was going to have to play out and with fucking Luca all over him, he wasn't about to waste time setting up and then taking a two hour detour for the meat, before heading back.

Christ. Times were easier back then.

Yesterday.

He smiled, wryly to himself. "How do you want to play this?" he asked.

"On my lead," she replied, absently.

"This it?" He said, turning into the road.

Bree looked at the signpost. "I guess." She'd never been there, just knew where it was.

Raymond arched his head forward, looking out the front window to the houses. "Nice," he said. He'd never liked coming into these sorts of places for business. It was bad enough at Bree's, but this was a different level. Cul-de-sac. All detached houses. Shit. If he'd thought about it, they could have set up in this dude's house.

"That one," she said, pointing.

Raymond pulled the car around. "You sure about this?"

Bree nodded. "It'll be fine."

After Raymond had pulled the car onto the driveway, Bree got out. She stepped over to the house, the lights on, downstairs. To the door. Rang the bell. She waited.

There was a shadow moving about. A little wobbly by the look of it. Looked like he'd been drinking.

He opened the door and looked at her. He didn't seem to recognise her at first. He glanced down her, wearing a long raincoat, concealing her body. A frown. Some spark of memory and then back up to her face. "Bree cheese," he said.

Cunt.

Bree dropped open the raincoat. Underneath she was wearing Gel's school uniform. "Still too dowdy?" she asked.

"Holy shit," he whispered.

"May I?" she asked.

Liam moved to the side and waved her in. "Changed your mind about the promotion, I see."

"That doesn't have to still be on the table," she purred, passing him. Dropping the coat from her shoulders to the floor. "I've moved on. I just thought I'd come by. See if I can fuck you this time. Show you how I make green now." She turned back to face him as he let the door close. His eyes wide, down her. On her tits. He liked the tightness of the uniform. The way the buttons nearly burst open as she breathed, pulling gaps, him seeing her flesh beneath.

"So why now?" he said. He pointed to the door on the right, and she led them into the living room.

"Seemed appropriate." She turned back to him. He was shuffling about. Caught off guard, but definitely up for it.

"So you want to fuck," he said. Not a question. He still thought he was going to be in charge. "I knew you wouldn't have had enough." He grinned. Wet. His lips looked rubbery, and his face drooped where he'd drunk too much.

She slipped up to him close. Her hand sliding down the front of his trousers. She was … less shy. Bolder. The other hand, up, under her skirt, to the syringe, nestled in the hem of her stockings. She popped the cap from it, as she slipped it around behind him. Stuck it in his arse.

"Hey," he said, pulling back, "easy." His eyes immediately glazed. "The fuck was that?" All came out like one word. *Thefuckwasthat*. He stumbled back a couple of steps, took a sofa to the knee and he was down. On the carpet. Head on the floor. His eyes were open, but he wasn't there anymore. Spittle drooling from the corner of his mouth. His lips opening and closing slowly.

Like a fish.

Bree snorted. She went back to the hall and pulled her coat back on. Then the front door. He was already leaning against the car waiting. She beckoned him over and he pushed himself off. Walked slowly to the house. Casual like.

He looked down at Liam. "So this is that piece of shit?"

"Uh huh." She crouched and rolled him.

"I got." Raymond bent down and roughly pulled Liam to his feet. He was still half awake. A slight change to the concoction of drugs and it made him seem like he was utterly shitfaced, not having completely blacked out.

Raymond had said that they rarely used it, as usually they were grabbing guys from alleyways and shit, but as they were grabbing someone from in their own home, it made sense. In case they got fronted by someone in the driveway.

Which they didn't.

The cul-de-sac was dead. They took Liam out the front door, and even dumped him straight in the boot.

Bree closed up the front door and they were away.

Only there for a matter of minutes.

Now Streaming

Raymond had hammered two bolts into the wall of the garage and Liam was hanging naked from them. He looked like a prisoner in medieval times, hands up above his head, head down, resting on his chest. Naked. The cold hard wall against his back.

Cameras in front of him.

Bree came halfway down the stairs. "Cold tonight," she said.

Raymond looked up from the laptop. "Good crowd though."

"Out with a bang. Did you tell them it was the last showing?"

"I didn't *tell* them. But it might have leaked." He looked at her, winked. "I wanted to get some of the juices flowing. Maybe entice back some of the high rollers. See if we can't make bank this time. For all of us."

Bree crossed to Liam. "He's awake."

"Yeah. We can start anytime."

"So what … Finish here, back to yours, pick up the bags and away?"

"Pretty much." I want to stop down one of the riverbanks somewhere and lose the laptops and cameras. One of the old fishing spots. Won't be anyone down there this time of year, and no one will be able to get shit off the lappies after they've been in the river for four months, and probably frozen over."

"Man with a plan," she said. "I like it." The house he'd found in the South of France was certainly big enough for her to have a room for a few weeks. They seemed more than happy to take her along for the ride, too. She looked at Liam. And she had no qualms about doing this.

Gel hit the stairs. "Ready," she said, pulling on her uniform hat. "What do you think?"
Raymond looked from the meat to her. "Beautiful," he said.
"Hot," Bree cut in.
She giggled. Loved the compliments, especially from Raymond. She went to him and leant down, looking at the screens. "Looks good."
"I don't recognise some of the names." Raymond jabbed his finger at a couple of the faces. "A few I do."
"What about Luca?" she asked.
"I don't see him." His eyebrows up.
"No." Gel knew that didn't mean a lot. He was able to find them at the last place. Fuck it, it wasn't a secret that they were doing this. How could it be? Fuck. Maybe he was getting laid tonight and won't have noticed them.
"Showtime," Raymond said.
Gel looked to him. He was looking at the meat. She turned her look to that instead. His head was up. He was looking around confused. Had a ball gag in, what with him able to identify Bree on camera.
She certainly didn't need that sort of trouble.
"And we have … nipples for five hundred."
"Ooh," said Gel. "We don't get that very often."

Liam was struggling, his feet still on the ground able

to take his weight—at the moment—as Bree held the knife under his nose. "Beautiful, isn't it?" It was a big thing. Rambo type effort. Very shiny at the moment. He was staring at it. His body stilled. He looked from the knife to her, and tried to say something. *Mmmmuuffggrr. Fnfnff oojefd.* "What's that sweetie?" she said, leaning in, safe from any biting attempts because of the gag. "You're sorry you raped me?" She looked up into his eyes. He was pleading with them. Afraid. Lost. "Is that it, is that what you're saying, because I can't understand." She smiled. "Or not? Were you saying it would turn you on if I did all the things the nice man with the laptop says?" She even put on a proper girly voice for that last bit. He screamed under the gag, thrashing again.

Obviously that wasn't it.

Oh, well.

She grinned at him. Held the flat of the blade to his skin just below the nipple. His moob holding the thing outwards. And it was hard. Probably the cold. Still. It made it an easy target. "Because you changed me," she said, sliding the knife slowly and carefully against his flesh. The sharp of the blade cutting through the fine hairs of his chest.

He was weeping.

Tears jerked down his face, changing direction each time he shook. And he was shaking plenty.

Bree cupped his balls—for the camera—and then she pushed the blade, flat, to a slight angle, and up, through the flesh, the circle of his nipple dropping off, spapping to the floor at their feet. He was screaming in the gag. Like a baby. Blood spat weakly from the wound, like he had no pressure in his body.

She twisted his balls. The pressure sure as shit wasn't down there. When she released his balls, his legs buckled, floppy, and he hung from his hands. "You pathetic cunt," she said, raising her knee hard into his chest. He stood back up, twisting and curling in some shit attempt as escape.

Gel was laughing at him. Deriding him. Belittling him. Teasing him like a cuck in a sex video. *Your willy is pathetic*, she was saying through the laughs. *But not as pathetic as you*.

Bree took the second nipple, her hand flat on his chest, pushing him back to the wall and she cut it off quickly. Blood running down him, slow. Onto his belly, just reaching his hips, into his hair, when she stepped to the kit and took the salt. Brought it over and showed him. "Nothing personal," she hissed, too low for the mic to pick up. He was shaking his head. Whining under the mask. She emptied some of the salt into her gloved palm and slapped it to the wound on the right, smushing it in.

And as he howled, a bloom of pleasure did too, in Bree.

Raymond squinted, watching the glee Bree took in the salting. It wasn't something they felt the need to do often. Usually just something Gel used when the meat pissed her off. He hissed some air in through his teeth, then turned his attention back to the screen. Some dude was jerking himself off, right there in the camera. Fucking hell. Raymond glanced to the girls again. He could see the appeal, he supposed. Fucking weirdos. Then back again. To a different screen. He wondered if Luca was there. Somewhere. Waiting to fucking taunt him again.

Joke was on him though. This was it. In less than eight hours the three of them would be at the airport. Probably eating an overpriced breakfast and people watching. Gel liked to people watch.

He read the next message. Called across, "Eat a finger. One thou." He looked back to the screen. "Nice," he muttered.

Bree was already at the kit.

Gel held his head up, while Bree used the shears to take a pinky. He was crying and screaming. Weak in the legs. Pissed himself as soon as she took the finger. There must have been something there inside him that told him that this was it. Something about cutting off the fingers that made it more *final*, somehow. Weird that cutting his nipples off hadn't done that. Bree was bending down, arse at the camera and picking up his finger. She brushed it off like the seven second rule applied when eating your own body parts, and then rose, legs spread like a gymnast.

Gel pulled the fastener open on the back of the gag and yanked it out his mouth. He was making such a palaver of everything he failed to shut his mouth so as to not eat his own finger. When Bree had stuffed the finger in his mouth, he still didn't do anything to stop Gel pushing the ball gag back in, in effect sealing the finger in there.

Then she did the gag strap back up.

He was choking. Gagging a little. He'd realised what he had in his mouth. Eyes wild. He was shaking his head, like he had a choice.

Silly boy.

Gel stroked his throat, encouraging him to swallow. She said, "If you eat it, we'll let you go. You've only lost one thing that's of any real use to you. And I'm sure you can live without one little finger." Her hand dropped to his cock, she took it in a fist. "There are worse things to lose."

He coughed and spluttered in the gag, around it, but he did it.

He actually swallowed the fucking finger.

Bree shook her head. "Jesus wept," she muttered. Fucking loser. She looked to Raymond for the next instruction. Listened to him gagging. He was throwing up in his mouth. Coughing. Snorting. Fucker was going to drown in his own puke if he wasn't careful. She cleared her throat. Took his attention from the screen.

"Sorry," he said. "Glitchy. We have twelve hundred for a knee cap—just one, shattered."

Bree nodded, turned back and looked at Gel. Offering her the chance to have a go.

"This boy's all yours if you want him."

Bree smiled. "Cheers, babe." She got the lump hammer from the kit and gave it a swing testing the weight.

Liam was flapping about in a panic.

Bree went and stood at his side. Lifted the mallet up. Lowered it slowly, making sure she was going to hit the right spot.

Raymond stared at the screen. There were about fifteen people in the audience at the moment. That was fine. One or two of them had dropped off a minute or two ago. But something didn't *feel* right.

The meat screamed like someone had just jammed a felled tree up his arsehole, and Raymond looked up. His kneecap, shattered, blood gushing from it. He'd clenched up so much due to the pain that his teeth had shattered on the ball gag, loosening it enough to let some of the sound out.

He glanced back to the screen. Gel should be able

to take care of that. No one had bid on the next thing. He'd only give them a few more seconds then he'd poke them. They didn't have the time nor the luxury to be dicking around today.

One of the screens cut out. Quickly replaced with another.

And the next.

Raymond's face dropped as he saw ... all the clients were dropping out and they were being replaced ... the replacement screens were of the same person. Leaning back in the shadows.

"Hello, Raymond," he said.

The screen filling with feed from Luca. He leant forward in his seat, the light casting deep shadows over his now clear face. "Fuck me over, would you?" he typed in.

Raymond looked at the words. Shit. Luca had hacked the Red Room. Fucker had closed them down.

That was when he heard it.

Sirens.

Chapter 33

"Pack up," Raymond barked. He typed, frantic, at the keyboard. "They're coming for us," he shouted.

The words appeared on the screen. *Thought you could skip out on me, did you? I've sent you over a little gift. You might want to be careful with them. They're not strippers, if you get my drift.*

Gel was already at the door. "Fuck," she shouted. "Coppers."

Cunt. Raymond finished typing in the code to the prompt and hit return. He picked up the laptop. Pulled the wires from it, killing the camera. "Kill him," he barked, waving the machine across the room to the meat.

Bree looked stunned. She turned. Looked at the kit. She was in shock. What the fuck was happening? They can't get caught. They had it all planned out.

"*In your hand*," Raymond shouted.

She looked down at the lump hammer. Fuck. Yes. She turned, raising it up like God damned Mjolnir. The square of metal hit Liam straight on the nose. The bone splintered and broke, his skin split. Blood rained out of him like he was a tap freshly turned on. She pulled the hammer back, up, again. She swung impaling it into his face. The bone structure collapsing. The hammer coming to a rest in the squishy mire of his brain. His body twitching like he was tweaking on the dance floor of some shitty fucking club.

Gel ran from the door. "What do we do?" she screamed.

Raymond thrust the laptop into her hands. "Take this. Out the back."

"What?" she screamed.

He stopped. The room freezing in the moment, even Bree stopped staring at Liam and brought her look to the two of them. Raymond, Gel, both holding the laptop. "You both have to go. It's the only way." His eyes flickered down to the laptop. "Take it. Make him sorry."

Gel was shaking her head. "No," she was saying. "No. What are you saying?"

Bree stumbled to her side. She took Gel's arm and pulled her away from Raymond towards the back door. Gel pulled back trying to get herself free, she *had* to help Raymond, but he was already running to the door. Out to the car.

He hurried over. The cast of the night cut with the lights of the police cars. Flashing over the sides of the buildings. Turning the corner into the garages. He grabbed the can of petrol from the boot and ran back to the building, twisting the cap off as he headed for the door. The police cars pulling up behind him. The Mondeo the only thing between him and them.

"Stop," one of them was shouting. "*Police.*"

Raymond tossed the open petrol can into the mess of computer equipment. The routers. Hard Drives. Satellite broadcast encryptors. The petrol gushed from it.

He dug his hand in his pocket and pulled Gel's lighter. Flicked it into life and then tossed it to the petrol. Just as the police reached the door.

The fumes took first. *Whump*. The evidence. The

data. Everything that connected the three of them together with the Red Room gone in a second. The flames tore through the building, as Raymond staggered away from the fire. He reached the door, out to the dirt outside. His legs taken from him, people crashing into him. He was on the floor before he knew it. His ears ringing with the bright sound of nothing but the explosion. Then … *eeeeeee*.

Someone was shouting at him. Someone else shouted, "Well stand on his fucking head, Davis." His arms twisted back, behind him. Pain burning in his shoulders. Some cunt was standing on his fucking head. He cried out. Tried to move a little. Everything hurt, as he felt cuffs snap on him.

He was dragged from the front of the burning building. Dumped onto the cracked tarmac. Face down. Someone kneeling between his shoulder blades. Couldn't breathe properly.

"There's still someone in there," one of them shouted.

"No," he tried to say. "Don't. He's already dead." But the words came out as little more than a wheeze. He looked up. The floor above was aflame. There was nothing but fire coming from the building. The internal floor crashed down, turning the building into little more than a chimney. An incinerator.

The police dragged him up to the car. Pushing him against it.

An older copper. Looked haggard and tired. "We got you, you bastard," he was saying, over and over as they pushed him in the car.

Gel stopped and looked back, but Bree grabbed her arm. The two of them in the fields behind the garages. One in each divot created by huge tractor tyres.

"Come on," Bree barked.

Gel had tears streaked down her face. Looking back. The light in the sky from the fire, the blue lights bouncing from the smoke around it. "Raymond," she said.

"He'll be fine," Bree dragged her forward. "We have to go." She stopped trying. Stopped and twisted Gel to face her. "We have to go. It's what he wanted." She had snot on her lips.

Nice.

But she nodded. Stumbled forward into the darkness. Up the embanked side of the field. Towards the top. "Where the fuck are we?"

"It's okay," Bree said, pushing herself up next to Gel. "We're not *that* far from mine."

Gel managed to snort out a laugh. "I hope not," she said. "You're dressed as a bloody school girl and I'm a fucking Nazi." Then she blubbed more, heaving air in as she struggled to keep her footing in the mud.

They reached the top of the field and Bree led them to the side, running along the top of the field, parallel to the road, hidden by trees, cars zipping past without their roof lights on. A fire engine, as they reached the edge of the field. Bree took them around the back of the three houses there. On the other side they were within running distance of a housing estate.

If the police weren't looking for them, then they could get some distance in the alleyways.

"Where are we going?" Gel wheezed.

"*Mine.*"

Gel looked her down. "We breaking in, or do you have pockets in that thing?" She wiped the snot from her face with the arm of the SS uniform.

"I've got one of those fake stones with a spare in, around the side."

Gel raised her eyebrows. "Right."

The two of them ran across the road when the street was empty and into the estate, hurrying into the alleys, disappearing into the night.

Chapter 34

Britain's Most Prolific Serial Killer – We Got Him. Gel pushed her phone away from her, across the kitchen table. She stared across the table for a moment. Looking at the nothing between her and the laptop.

Bree came in behind her. "What does the news say?" She pushed the button on the kettle to reheat the water.

"They've fingered him for just about every body found in the country in the last two years. Gonna go down forever."

"*Shit*," she responded. Gel had been staying with her for the last few nights. The two of them had gotten back to hers, changed, and jumped in the car. Going to Gel and Raymond's and collecting their things, knowing that once the filth had been all over the place, they were never going to get back in. By the time they'd taken all the bags packed for the South of France, there was no trace of either of them.

The police were never going to know their involvement. Not unless they found the Red Room footage, and Raymond had taken care of most of that. As long as no one from the audience came forward, no one would ever know.

Gel raised the lid on the laptop. Looked at the screen. She slowly closed it again. The battery was at forty percent and she still didn't know why she had it.

The charger hadn't arrived from Ebay yet. So she didn't want to waste it.

But she would keep it safe.

Bree pushed a coffee in front of her. "Now what?" she asked. She didn't want to say it, but the money they had wasn't going to last forever.

Three Months later

Bree sat in the car in the car park outside Felway Max. The prison on the island just off the mainland. Like Alcatraz, but with a bridge. So, *shit* Alcatraz.

She was playing Angry Birds on some Android thing she'd forgotten she had.

Gel was in there, visiting Raymond for the first time. She was going to be giving him shit left and right about how the trial went down. They'd pushed for a quick one. Gotten it, too, and to Gel's surprise Raymond plead guilty on fucking all of it.

Bree knew he was going to, of course. But she hadn't said anything. She knew he'd do it to close the lid on it all. Make sure they never came for her. She'd seen it in his eyes. The way he looked at her. He'd have done anything to protect her.

She glanced up as the crates on the screen exploded. Gel was coming across the road, so she stuffed the machine into her handbag and tossed it over to the back seat. Bree could see the tears lining Gel's face all the way across the car park.

Gel almost ran into a car passing, not paying enough attention, before getting to the car and climbing in. She sat in silence for a couple of minutes, and Bree didn't speak, letting her gather her thoughts before spouting anything out.

Then she said, "He wants us to go to the South of

France without him."

Well, it wasn't like he could come, was it? He'd been sentenced to life without the possibility of parole. "Okay," Bree whispered, carefully not committing to it either being a good, nor a bad idea. See how Gel was taking it first.

"Which I'm on board with."

That did surprise Bree.

"But we have something to do first."

CHAPTER 35

Raymond typed frantically, pushing the backdoor open on Luca's connection. He glanced over to Bree, smashing the meat's face in. Gel at the door. He could tell by the look on her face, this was it. This was the end, one way or another. The door opened. The encryption came down. Luca was transmitting from a house. Up, north of London. The address, right there on the screen, smooshed into the middle of the code. He slapped the laptop shut and took it, yanking the power cord out, tossing it to the side. He hurried over to Gel. Pushed it into her hands.

Go. Go now.

Gel sat in the car. She had the laptop on her lap, looking at the aerial view of Luca's pad, while the house itself was only a few hundred yards away. "We could always go into business dealing on the dark web," she said. "Apparently it pay's rather well."

Bree grunted. "Sure." She looked from the house on the horizon to Gel. "So bored." They'd been there less than two hours, but she'd had it. She just wanted to get on with it.

"He'll be here," Gel said.

After seeing Raymond in the prison, he'd told her how to extract the address from the code. Told her to take revenge on him. He was a danger. He might never let the two of them go, not with what he knew, and how he felt. Fuck him up, and flee the country. It was the only way to guarantee the safety of the two of them.

Just then, Luca's Land Rover passed them, sitting in the mouth of an off-road. He didn't see them. Certainly wasn't looking.

Not for a car, sitting there in the middle of nowhere with two SS uniform clad girls. Waiting.

Luca was a fool. He didn't do anything with any care. You would think that a man with his reach and his power would basically be a Bond villain, but no. He seemed to think himself untouchable. Or, in the sticks and no one would find him.

Well, Raymond had.

Gel opened the kitchen door carefully. No security lights. No alarms. Stupid fucker. She had half the gear in a holdall, over her shoulder. Bree had the other half.

The house was huge. It was a surprise, but he seemed to live there alone. Which was just as well, because all said and done Gel wasn't too worried about collateral damage in the Luca household, if you know what she meant.

The two of them closed up the door in the kitchen. Dropped the bags down silently and went around the ground floor.

There was a fucking poolroom, and a *pool* room.

Bree snorted some disgust. "And we're scrabbling for cash?"

"Fucker," Gel said in agreement. She eyed the pool table and the cues and the balls. Hm. Then she said, "This'll do."

Now Streaming

Luca opened his eyes, bleary. Pain sloshing around in there like there was too much blood in his head, and not enough anywhere else. He knew he was naked, because he was naked when he got into bed, and he could feel it. You know, like the bed clothes had fallen off. But he had a spiking pain in his lower back, and was clearly laying on something far harder than his bed. "Fuck," he whispered, "what the fuck happened?"

"You had an accident on the stairs."

He snapped his eyes properly open, and lifted his head. It was difficult. What the fuck? He was strapped to the pool table in the poolroom. Naked. Spread eagle. Back stinging like he'd been beaten with something. "Who the fuck are you?" he asked.

The woman stepped closer. Shit. Then he recognised her. "Gel," he whispered. "Raymond's whore."

She slapped him. "Fuck you."

She turned away and the other one came up. It was her, from the stream. The Red Room. The one they'd picked up as a third near the *end of their career*. "What the fuck do you think you're playing at? Do you know what my boys will do to you if you so much as lay a finger on me?" He laughed. Felt his cock stirring. "You might as well just fuck me and leave." He looked over to the two of them, stood together now, watching in silence. "You don't have the balls to hurt me." He glanced down at his cock. Engorging. Hm. That didn't seem right.

Gel sucked air in. "I see the drugs are kicking in," she said. She went behind the laptop on the little round table that always sat between the stools in a poolroom for some reason and opened The Red Room. There were all the people that got turned out of the Red Room they had to close because of Luca.
All invited to a private room, for free. As a thank you for their patronage, and an apology for cutting the last showing short.
"Okay," she typed in. She wasn't very good at this bit. Raymond was so much more in charge. Confident. "No charge, but this one needs to hurt." She glanced over to him. Writhing about trying to free himself, cock wiggling about humorously.
"Burn him."
"Burn him," she echoed. A glance to Bree.

Bree shrugged. That was new. "Okie Dokie," she said. "One second." She smiled at Luca. Hurried off, around to the kitchen. The two of them had plenty of time to acquaint themselves with the property while he was … sleeping. She opened a couple of drawers, looking for something suitable. Found a baby blowtorch with a portable smoking machine. "Awesome," she muttered to herself.
She returned to the poolroom and fired the torch over him.
"No," he said. "I know who you are. I can tell everyone your names. They'll all know."
"You think that *matters* anymore you *fucking cunt*." Gel strode to the table. "Tell them. Think it's

going to stop us?"

Bree waved the torch in front of his eye line. He closed his eyes, like she was going to burn them, but as Gel strode back to the screen, Bree drew a line with the harsh blue flame of the blow torch down the side of Luca's leg. He screamed out in agony, but all that did was encourage Bree to run it back up his leg, the other way, blackening and blistering skin, making it pop and fry. *Sssss*.

He tried so hard to wriggle away like a worm.

"Teeth," said Gel.

"You want?" she replied.

Gel shook her head, attention on the screen.

Bree went to the kit. Smaller, as they had to lug it in, and the whole lot was staying there this time. She grabbed the pliers and took them to him. He'd clamped his mouth shut. Wet streaks down his face. Head shaking. *No. No, you're not getting to my teeth*.

"You know," Bree said. "It'll hurt a lot less if you actually comply. At least with this thing." She waved the pliers over his face. Still his head shook. "Ah," she said, turning away, "the hard way." She dropped the pliers down and picked up the claw hammer. Took that to him instead. "Too late now," she teased.

Then she used the claw side of the hammer, banging it against his closed mouth, tearing the skin open, chipping the teeth first and then cracking them. Splinters and shards coming off in his mouth as it filled with blood. The teeth breaking off at weird angles and cutting his gums, his cheeks. He wailed out and she got it right in, turning and twisting the hammerhead, breaking his back teeth, tearing his gums to shit. Yanking the hammer from his mouth, a part of his tongue came out with it. Plopped on the pool table. He turned his head to the side allowing the blood to drain from him. Pooling, if you will, on the pool table.

Gel was watching.

Gel looked at the screen. She wasn't grinning. Didn't take pleasure in this. She just wanted it done. And she wanted it done in the most violent way possible. "You'll have to wait for that one," she typed, replying to a request. The next one simply said, "Elbows." She nodded. Got herself in front of the camera. Bent forward, to let them see her panties. Then up, "Elbows," she relayed to Bree. She went to the kit herself and grabbed the mallet. Swung it hard and quick, down onto Luca's elbow. The bones broke, parting under the skin. Dislocating.

He screamed. Oh, how he screamed.

The pain was like a thousand fires raging in his arm. Starting like a shard of ice, it morphed to burning heat, and finally this ever present stabbing. "Please," he screamed through the blood in his mouth, his voice unrecognisable. "I'll do anything."

Gel leaned over him. "I want Raymond back," she hissed, "you cunt."

She was rounding the table, then.

The burning sensation in his leg had dulled to a crackling feeling. Lost to the pain in his face. His head. He felt like his eyes were going to swell up and pop. Like he might be drowning in blood. His jaw might be hanging off.

She slammed the fucking hammer onto him, and another, new, pain flared in his body. He banged his head back. A sheet of white lightning crossing his eyes and taking his feeling. And just for a second there was nothing. Like his body had just closed the doors on it and shut it out. But all in a rush it returned, every nerve ending in his body screaming in unison like he was being buried in the sun.

Then a darkness.

Burning darkness. Somewhere in an unconscious state, but still able to feel the torment.

Always feeling the torment.

Gel stepped back and looked down at him. "Fucker's blacked out."

Bree got the salts and waved them under his nose. He groaned, but didn't wake. Gel rocked his head to the side so he wouldn't drown in his own mouth blood. Then she went to the laptop. "We're just taking a short break. Back in five." She left the camera on, but her and Bree left the room, letting the audience see his broken body. Bloody on the table.

Still had a hard on, though.

Chapter 36

The two of them went upstairs. "Time?" Bree asked.

"Yeah. I wanted to do so much more, but he's clearly not up to it." They went to his bedroom and both stripped naked. Into the en suite and turned the shower on.

Gel stepped in while Bree looked over her hair, making sure there weren't any bits of broken teeth in there. Gel washing the blood off herself. The water in the base of the shower, running pink.

She stepped out, and swapped with Bree.

The two of them cleaning themselves off in silence.

They returned to the bedroom and dressed in the clothes from the second bag. Clean, casual. Nothing to them. Then they returned downstairs.

Collected nothing. Their bags, tickets for their flights, everything they needed, in the boot of the car.

This was how it was to end.

NOW STREAMING

Jilly watched. It was getting boring now. They'd been gone for nearly twenty minutes. She tapped her fingernail on the desk. Sure it was free, but come on. She wanted to know what the end game was.

Then she saw movement in the background of the feed.

The meat was moving his head, had been for a few minutes, and she could hear him, moaning and groaning. Such a turn on, right? But they were back. A bit of a blur being so far away from the table, but it looked like they'd changed clothes.

She smiled. That was a change.

They were doing something. Something carefully. She leant closer into the screen. The darkness of the office around her. She could hear her kids in the next room. She was going to have to put up sound proofing wasn't she? How could she be expected to work from home while her kids were making such a racket, and why the fuck wasn't her husband dealing with it?

She sat back, denying herself any sexual gratification watching this—not while she could hear her kids, anyway.

The two women. They were doing something with bottles. Pouring something around the table now.

Then over him. His junk anyway. He had a nice cock. Big and hard. She hoped they were going to cut it off. Poor guy seemed well out of it, so he didn't react to what they were doing.

Then the first one left. She went out of shot. Gone. She was the newer of the two. This wasn't Jilly's first rodeo after all.

The second stood there. She whispered something to the meat.

Jilly would have given anything to know what you say to the meat just before you end things.

Then she sparked a lighter.

Oh, my.

She walked away, to the doorway of the room before dropping the lighter to the floor. Then she turned and left as fire wound its way from the door, following the path of the accelerant to the table, leaping up onto the table next to him, like a cat.

The flames licked his body, jumping to his torso, his cock and balls burning vividly on the screen.

Jilly sucked air in through her teeth, bit her lip, watching the meat cook. He was screaming and thrashing as his crotch and hips raged like a barbeque.

Yes.

He was making this heaving sound, as the flames crept up his torso, spitting onto the baize of the table, the whole platform becoming a pyre, quelling his screams, before dropping to the floor. The carpet this side of the table turning to fire.

Everything burning.

The screen crackled as the heat in the room did. Glass on the other side of the room—a trophy cabinet of some sort—cracked, then shattered.

The room filling with smoke as *everything* blazed.

Jilly breathed hard, excitement curling her toes.

Then the screen went black.

Stream ended

About the Author

Ash is a British horror author. He resides in the south, in the Garden of England. He writes horror that is sometimes fantastical, sometimes grounded, but always deeply graphic, and black with humour.

www.ashericmore.com

Printed in Great Britain
by Amazon